LIFE AFTER DEATH

Books by Angela Roquet

Return to Limbo City (A Lana Harvey Spin-off Series)
Life After Death
Shadow of Death
Death's Door (Summer 2022)
Tree of Death (Autumn 2022)
To the Death (Winter 2022)

Lana Harvey, Reapers Inc.
Graveyard Shift
Pocket Full of Posies
For the Birds
Psychopomp
Death Wish
Ghost Market
Hellfire and Brimstone
Limbo City Lights (short story collection)
The Illustrated Guide to Limbo City

Blood Vice
Blood Vice
Blood and Thunder
Blood in the Water
Blood Dolls
Thicker Than Blood
Blood, Sweat, and Tears
Flesh and Blood
Out for Blood

Spero Heights
Blood Moon
Death at First Sight
The Midnight District

Visit **angelaroquet.com** for a complete list of Angela's works.

LIFE AFTER DEATH

BOOK ONE OF

RETURN TO LIMBO CITY

ANGELA ROQUET

VIOLENT SIREN PRESS

LIFE AFTER DEATH

Copyright © 2021 by Angela Roquet

www.angelaroquet.com

Cover Art by Rebecca Frank

Edited by Chelle Olson of Literally Addicted to Detail

ISBN: 978-1-951603-57-1

For Paul and Xavier,
the center of my universe.

THE GOSPEL OF LANA

A grim summary of the original Lana Harvey, Reapers Inc. series.

IN THE BEGINNING...

Let's be real. It was a train wreck.

A few thousand years ago, a handful of original believers willed the deities and afterlives of Eternity into existence. The gods have been at odds ever since, bickering over the fates of the deceased and the soul matter that shapes our world beyond the grave.

The boundaries of the heavens and hells shifted at the whim of believers, encouraging wrathful deities to smite one another. It was a bloody affair. The War of Eternity raged on and on for the longest time.

But then, in the early seventh century, when my not-so-dearly departed ex-boss was out doing his thing, reaping souls and whatnot, he came across one of those original believers. Khadija.

Grim showed her the chaos and suffering beyond the grave, and she was compelled to help. As a rare original believer, Khadija had the power to stabilize the borders of the afterlives. She also forged the secret Throne of Eternity—an intangible connection to and command over the soul matter that flowed from the mortal realm to the afterlives. The lifeblood of Eternity.

Through this new bond, she created Limbo City, a neutral territory where Grim could broker peaceful negotiations between the gods. While he was at it, he also decided to take full credit for the feat and hid Khadija away in a secret pocket realm.

For her own safety, *I'm sure*. Such a peach, that Grim.

Anyway, the gods signed the peace treaty and agreed to end the War of Eternity, and the Afterlife Council was formed—with Grim in a neutral leadership role as their president. They determined a yearly date where the excess soul matter could be distributed in an organized and agreeable fashion, an event that came to be called the Oracle Ball.

A few centuries later, Grim convinced the council to repay his generous and mysterious efforts by allotting him a smidge of soul matter every hundred years to create extra reapers to help with his growing soul harvesting business. And, thus, Reapers Inc. was founded.

It was a cushy gig for ol' Death.

Until I came along and mucked things up.

Though I suppose that blame really belongs to Khadija. After a thousand years, she was ready to retire from the throne and turn it over to another original believer.

By then, Grim didn't go out in the field anymore, but he certainly wasn't about to entrust such a delicate—and advantageous—task to anyone else.

Cue the feet-dragging... for a few centuries.

Khadija, being the wise and intuitive soul that she was, took matters into her own hands. While whipping up the eighth generation of reapers in 1709, she baked a little something extra into my soul matter. I hadn't simply been made in Grim's image—I was his equal.

Like other reapers, I was immortal and had the innate ability to harvest souls. But unlike the others, I could see the potency of a soul in their aura. It was a neat little trick, helpful in identifying original believers. A skill Grim *definitely* didn't want anyone else to have. And, also, one that made my existence a breach of the peace treaty, which stipulated that no new deities would be created with the excess soul matter.

Deity felt too strong a word for someone with a skill that barely rivaled Superman's x-ray vision. But it made me *other*. Something more than the council had agreed to, which would have put both Grim and me in a sticky situation if anyone found out.

It seemed like something that should have been easy to hide. Hell, I hadn't even known I had this ability until three hundred years after the fact, when Khadija was good and sick of Grim's shit—and losing hers.

The soul matter was becoming harder to control. She was slipping, and a rogue island had popped up in the Sea of Eternity—one that rebel demons were using as their base.

There was also the issue of Khadija's husband losing patience in Jannah, the Islamic heaven. He sent the angel Maalik, the Keeper of Hellfire himself, to Limbo City to join the Afterlife Council and investigate the matter. I don't suppose breaking my heart had been on the list, but he managed that well enough, too. At least I got full custody of the pair of hellhounds he'd gifted me early in the relationship.

Back to the rebel demons and leaking soul matter...

When Grim realized he was between a headstone and a hard place, Khadija finally told him about me. I mean, he *knew* about me, just not that I was special. I hadn't been there to see his reaction, but I imagined it was probably a lot like one of those Jerry Springer episodes where the guy finds out he's the father and is *not* thrilled about it.

And, of course, Grim still tried to keep the truth from me when he dropped the promotion of the century in my lap with no explanation, made all the more jarring by the fact that I ranked somewhere near the bottom of the reaper barrel. I was a low-risk harvester with a questionable number of soul violations due to my penchant for slipping souls bound for the Sea of Eternity into more desirable afterlives.

My BFF, Gabriel—yeah, *that* Gabriel—says I have a savior complex. Artemis calls it stray dog syndrome. I find any spark of goodness redeemable. And why not?

Atheists and agnostics had no afterlives to claim them, so their souls were dumped into the ghostly sea surrounding Limbo City, where they awaited being sucked up by the Three Fates Factory and reinstalled in the mortal realm. It seemed like such a waste—and an inconvenience, seeing as how reapers then had to sail across said sea to deliver the rest of their charges to their afterlives.

These less-than-Death-like tendencies of mine made a promotion sound more like an April Fool's joke. Nevertheless, Grim had tasked me and a small team of reapers that included my sailing partner Josie Galla, Grim's second-in-command Coreen Bendura, and Coreen's apprentice Kevin Kraus with harvesting an extra-high-risk soul. The job went sideways when demons pushed our mark's bus off the San Francisco Bay Bridge, and we had to take a little dip to retrieve his soul.

After that, Grim had finally let Maalik introduce me to Khadija to get the explanation I deserved. It also became clear that the demon rebels were in on our little mission to find a new soul for the Throne of Eternity.

And the Egyptian god Seth, a member of the Afterlife Council, was heading up the opposition.

Not everyone had been happy with the terms of the peace treaty, and the fading pantheons with shriveling territories were especially bitter. Some of the old gods handled the transition with more grace, merging lands and sharing their obligations to subjects and souls. Others resisted fiercely.

The Summerland Society had been after the Sphinx Congress for centuries to unite their subcommittees and share their seats on the Afterlife Council. Horus managed to postpone that fate in exchange for working with Grim to seek out souls of ancient Egyptian origin, since the flow of spirits to Duat, the Egyptian underworld, had all but dried up. Grim said he'd turn over the unsuitable souls for the Weighing of the Hearts Ceremony, and Horus agreed not to ask any questions about the one Grim intended to keep.

To Horus's disappointment, and Grim's relief, it'd only taken three harvests to find a replacement for Khadija. Unfortunately, the casualties included Coreen Bendura—gutted by hellcats during a demonic battle at sea—and Wosyet, a minor Egyptian goddess-slash-spy for Seth, beheaded by me with my fancy new battle axe.

That was what she got for trying to nab my soul. Well, not *my* soul—reapers don't have souls. The soul I had been tasked to collect. Winston, formerly known as Tutankhamun. King freakin' Tut.

So, Khadija drank Meng Po's special memory-erasing tea and headed off to Firdaws Pardis for her long-awaited retirement, and Winston drank a tea to peel back his past lives so he could take the reins of Eternity. Mission accomplished.

You'd think my life would have gone back to normal, right?

Ha.

No such luck.

Turned out, when the boss gave an undeserving peon a fancy new job description, people noticed. Important people.

Before I could roll a coin, I was in over my head.

Horus did not like that Grim had one of his favorite pharaohs on a leash. And while he didn't *exactly* know what had happened to Wosyet, he made an educated guess.

Giving her the literal axe was another *ruh-roh* regarding the peace treaty and reaper rights—or lack thereof. Not surprisingly, Grim decided to sweep that little mishap under the rug and failed to report it to the Afterlife Council.

Horus didn't give a crap about Wosyet, but knowledge of her demise made it super easy for him to blackmail me into an illegal side job. *What can I say?* I liked my head attached to my neck.

That two-faced son of a jackal tasked me with seeking out more original believers—on the down-low—with some banned tracking bracelets. The idea was to have a new soul ready to replace Winston in a hundred years when Horus wanted to take the kid home to Duat.

Horus also campaigned for my promotion to the Posy Unit, a specialty group of reapers that harvested mass souls from natural disasters, warzones, and epidemics. The move put me in contact with the most souls to comb through in search of original believers. Though it wasn't a great environment for training an apprentice—which I was in no way qualified to have. But with Coreen gone, Kevin in need of a new mentor, and Grim hating my guts, I was a prime target.

Luckily, Josie was there to pick up my slack and helped school Kevin in all sorts of things. *All* sorts of things.

Their canoodling was a welcome distraction. With Horus making my placement on the Posy Unit a council matter, many were eager to secure a favor for their vote. This attention did not escape the notice of the rebel demons.

Which was how my apartment ended up in flames, and I found myself recovering from a nasty burn at Meng Po's temple along the wooded coast of Limbo. She took the opportunity to barter her favorable vote in exchange for me speaking to Grim on her behalf, to remind him of her desire to alter the Three Fates' soul recycling process with her tea.

Soon after, another council member, Jesus's sister Holly Spirit, extended an invitation for me to take up residency in one of her lush condos at Holly House—because *landlord* is just a page before *leverage* in the dictionary.

And then there was Cindy Morningstar, Lucifer's daughter, who was also on the council and looking for good press. Which reapers being attacked by rebel demons on the job most definitely was *not*. Cindy requested that I take a two-week demon defense training course with Beelzebub, Lord of the Flies.

I'd been blowing off the Prince of Demons since I was already swamped with homework from the Reaper Academy. I'd let Josie talk me into Grace Adeline's wandering souls course—that my creep of an ex, Craig Hogan, was also taking. Plus, there was the mentoring class that Grim had signed me up for. Still, the blistery handprint around my neck made me think it was time to give demon defense the old college try.

I hadn't counted on falling in love with Bub in the process. But I did. Hard.

At the same time, I was falling *out* of love with Maalik. The angel was a firm believer in rules, and my very existence broke too many of them. I couldn't tell him what I was doing for Horus, nor why I was fighting for a fancy promotion that I clearly did not want. And I was so beyond his patronizing damsel-in-distress treatment.

To top it off, the demon rebels weren't done with me yet, and they'd recruited Craig.

I passed my classes with flying colors, only to be attacked in the street by the fury Tisiphone and my douche of an ex. I took quite the beating before discovering another *grim* talent when my hands lit up like a Christmas tree, and I pulled Craig straight out of existence.

Pop *goes the weasel.*

Nothing more than soul matter scattered into the ether.

Even more alarming? No one seemed to remember him. If only I could have forgotten Craig, too. His death—unexistence… whatever—rattled me. His face haunted my nightmares.

But I sallied forth, and when the Afterlife Council voted, I landed the Posy promotion… and was named the unit's new captain.

Totally unheard of for an eighth-generation reaper.

Clearly a fluke.

If Josie's roommate, Jenni Fang, hadn't immediately been announced as Grim's new second-in-command, I shudder to think what rumors might have grown fangs and taken a bite out of my ass.

The new gig as captain was an adjustment, but I put my scythe to the grindstone and made the most of it. Did a bang-up job, too, if I do say so myself. It was an easier feat to manage without Gabriel dragging me off to Purgatory Lounge every other night.

My angelic drinking buddy was not thrilled with my new brimstone beau, which made him a big fat hypocrite since he was dating a demon himself. Both of our hellish heartthrobs were on the Hell Committee, working directly under Cindy Morningstar, a detail that would later cause problems for both of us.

Once again, I expected that my world would return to some semblance of normal. For a minute there, it did, despite all the changes in my life—the fancier job title, the swanky living situation, an apprentice, and a lusty demon consort.

But the calm before the storm never lasts long.

The rebels sank their talons into everything, infiltrating the city and luring reapers and deities to the dark side. They abducted Jenni Fang and put the shape-shifting trickster god Loki in her place. They stole Hades' Cap of Invisibility, Atropos's shears, and Ammit's crocodile headdress.

But we prevailed. We rescued Jenni from literal and figurative hell. We reclaimed the stolen goods and brought a mountain down on the heads of those who tried to stand in our way.

There was hardly time to lick our wounds before Eternity threatened to rip apart at the seams once again, though. The rebels took Grim's brother Hypnos hostage. Though the boss man acted as if it were the end of the world, that one was *waaay* down on my list of things most likely to launch the apocalypse.

Turned out, King Tut wasn't an original believer, after all. He'd only restored the faith after his predecessor had tried to destroy it. As a result, Winston was already slipping, losing his hold on the soul matter.

Good thing I'd finally stumbled upon a suitable soul to take his place.

Only… I really wasn't looking forward to being *terminated* once Grim found out. He'd seemed perfectly content going back to pretending like he was the ringmaster of this circus and letting the peanut shells pile up on the tent floor for another millennium.

Without consulting anyone—Grim, me, or otherwise—Winston gave up the throne to the new soul, Naledi. But as luck would have it, he was smitten with her, so he decided to stick around and run interference with Grim. Which meant I got to keep breathing, at least for a little while.

I liked breathing.

Though maybe a bit less so after Beelzebub ripped my heart out by joining the rebels, and Lorelei, one of Eurynome's hench-sirens, killed Josie. Seth had recruited the Greek mermaid goddess and made her a general among the water-dwelling rebels.

Josie's death and Beelzebub's betrayal almost did me in. At least Gabriel had been there to catch me when I fell. But there wasn't enough Ambrosia Ale or John Wayne movies in the world to erase the hurt this time.

The revelation that Bub had been working undercover with the rebels on Cindy Morningstar's orders only mildly lessened my misery. But the truth hadn't prevented his summer home in Tartarus from being demolished or his houseboat on the Styx from being torched. It hadn't kept his demon butler Jack from being accosted and having to be taken to Meng Po's with a cracked horn. Nor me from having to take over instructing his demon defense course at the Reaper Academy.

Then there was Kevin's hellfire addiction.

My apprentice had not handled Josie's death well. I didn't have a lot of room to talk. I hadn't even noticed that one of my hellhounds was pregnant until she popped out three helljack puppies—fathered by one of Anubis's jackals.

I was lacking as a mentor, and without Josie's help with Kevin, I couldn't seem to find a middle ground between paralysis and tough love for my apprentice. It had seemed insignificant with demons breathing down my neck and Eternity swirling around the proverbial drain.

Especially after Naledi went missing, and Winston lost his mind.

To make matters worse, the tracking bracelets Horus had given me to tag original believers weren't working. Anytime Naledi's pinged on the tracking compact, I arrived in time to find a different original believer, but not her.

Soon, Winston's hysteria drew Maalik's attention—like I really needed his nose in my business again. The overbearing angel threatened me into turning over the tracking compact in exchange for not telling Grim about the ol' switcheroo with the soul on the throne. Which meant my hands were tied.

With nothing more pressing to distract me, I was finally forced to take a hard look at what my negligence with Kevin had cost. I thought I'd seen rock bottom before. I hadn't even come close. The situation came to a head when the captain of the Nephilim Guard brought Kevin home after he'd ransacked the condo and sold Jenni's and my valuables for drugs.

I did my best to set him straight and give him the attention and direction he clearly needed. Then I ran off to make a trade with the rebels: Winston for the Lord of the Flies.

Bub's cover had been blown, and he was now their captive. The Witch of Endor had delivered a cryptic message, just for me, revealing the rendezvous location.

I didn't want to use Winston—and it hadn't been my idea. He was convinced that the rebels had Naledi and just didn't know who or what she was. Why else would she have disappeared and not told him? The trade was the only way to find out for certain *and* get my demon back. It wasn't an opportunity I could afford to turn down.

Though I still regretted what happened after.

Winston and I met with the rebels. We made the trade, narrowly avoiding an ambush, and I took Bub to safety on one of the sacred faerie isles in the Sea of Avalon. They only granted us sanctuary for a single night, but it was just as well.

The Oracle Ball was the next evening, and Seth and the Witch of Endor had big plans for Winston—the soul they assumed would give them absolute control of Eternity. The witch was a powerful necromancer, and with the Seal of Solomon, she could also control demons. In no time at all, the guests that had gathered on the rooftop of Reapers Inc. for the ball became her hostages.

That was when Naledi finally made a reappearance and announced herself to the world. She was too late to save Winston, but she stopped the Witch of Endor's reign of terror by ripping the heart from the woman's chest. And as soon as Grim put the pieces together, he almost ripped the heart from *mine*.

Jenni Fang saved me from that grisly fate, and Grim fled the city to escape the consequences of his secret having been exposed. The power he'd once held over Eternity now had a name and a face that he didn't recognize. It was no longer his to wield.

Gloating would have been petty. I'd love to say that was the reason I didn't, but the truth was, I had my own music to face.

Naledi's debut came with lots of questions, and my role and unsanctioned soul vision were soon revealed. There were other ways to discover a soul's potency, but none so convenient as my natural talent—which made me a threat. Not because I had any phenomenal cosmic powers, but because I was the only one who could glance at a soul and tell if *they* did.

The Afterlife Council demanded that Naledi strip me of my gift. Then, to prove I was worthy of their trust, they tasked me with dismantling the ghost market. The number of CNH—Currently Not Harvestable—souls spiked after the Second War of Eternity officially ended with Seth's disappearance, and the Witch of Endor's death. Displaced rebels made their living by stealing valuable souls and selling them on the ghost market. And if I couldn't stop them, the council was ready to *terminate* me the same way Grim had wanted to.

Bub's solution was to take our new houseboat through a portal to the mortal side and live on the lam, at large but together, like Bonnie and Clyde. Such a romantic. It seemed his name had been cleared just in time for mine to make Eternity's Most Wanted list.

But I was never one to go down without a fight. Besides, one of the missing souls was Jai Ling, Meng Po's assistant. In my many recent stays at the temple after getting the crap kicked out of me by demons, I'd grown fond of the girl. There was also Warren, the nephilim I'd purchased my fancy battle axe from, who was dying for me to try out the new soul gauntlet he'd designed.

Even so, my face had been in the news too much, plastered on the cover of *Limbo's Laundry* and the *Daily Reaper Report*. There was no way rebel demons would talk to me. A rebel reaper, on the other hand...

Tasha Henry, a soul harvester from my generation, had joined the rebels early on. Now, she was living on the streets of Limbo City, scavenging from dumpsters and hunted by the Nephilim Guard. Enlisting her help was no easy feat—especially after our paths had crossed the winter before, when she'd sabotaged a holly-jolly, high-profile harvest in Alaska.

The council did not approve of Tasha's involvement, but she proved essential in taking down the ghost market and saving the missing souls. So, when the council gathered to decide her fate—right after they nearly voted *off with my head*, despite my success—I had no choice but to help her escape.

I got away with it, too, though the powers that be had their suspicions. Things became… chilly in Limbo City.

I put in my notice at Holly House and shacked up with Bub in Tartarus. The manor had been rebuilt, and the hellhounds preferred roaming the surrounding desert to being cooped up in the condo anyway. Plus, I liked having my demon all to myself. It didn't matter if home was where the hellfire burned, so long as I had the Lord of the Flies in my bed.

Kevin moved into the captain's cabin of our ship, and our third roommate, Jenni Fang, kept the condo since she could afford it by herself. When Grim hadn't returned, she'd taken over as Reapers Inc.'s new president and was ready to make some waves. I just wish I hadn't been in the splash zone.

Since so many reapers had joined the rebels or died in the war, we were working overtime to keep up with the surplus of harvests. Jenni and Naledi had petitioned the council to create a new generation earlier than scheduled, but in the meantime, Jenni had another *brilliant* idea.

She ripped Ellen Aries, a first-generation reaper whom Grim had made his secretary when she proved ill-suited for harvesting, from behind her desk and thrust her into the field. And since the council had decided to dissolve the Special Ops Unit I'd been put in charge of for the ghost market assignment, who better to shadow Ellen during her first week on the job?

Babysitting duty was made even more tedious by Ellen's whining and incompetence. Just when I'd resigned myself to a mind-numbing week—or three, considering how things were going—I came face-to-face with Vince Hare, a reaper who had reportedly been terminated a hundred years earlier. I was so shocked that I didn't realize until it was too late that he was there to steal one of my harvests. The prick.

Relaying this information to Jenni Fang proved useless. She didn't believe me. Or maybe she didn't *want* to believe me.

Things were peaceful. The city was rebuilding in the aftermath of the war, and the council was finally assimilating to Jenni's presence, as well as Naledi's. Digging up graves was a bad idea right now—one Jenni assumed I had suggested just to reinvent the Special Ops Unit that came with more pay and prestige.

That didn't stop me from digging around on my own time, though. Of course, everything I found only led to more questions and more heartache.

My late mentor, Saul Avelo, had been tasked with hunting down Vince Hare. Instead, he'd let him go. Shortly after, Saul had died in the line of duty—or so the papers claimed. The truth was much messier.

When the ghost market got rounded up, not all the missing souls from the factory had been accounted for. As it turned out, many of them had defected and hitched a ride with Vince to the mortal side, where they were preparing for a rebellion against Limbo City. But before Vince, Saul had been their leader.

It hurt, realizing how little I'd known my mentor. After my apprenticeship had ended, we'd grown distant, but I would have never imagined Saul capable of something like this. Gabriel hadn't known either, and they'd been friends for even longer.

Like Jenni, Naledi had been making some changes of her own, gathering more original believers in the throne realm to form her Apparition Agency. The council resisted this move, though it seemed even more necessary after learning what Vince and his army of souls had planned. But Naledi was less concerned with Vince. Grim Thanatos was paving the way for his return.

Seth had been found—or what was left of him, anyway.

And Naledi feared a similar fate for the souls in Vince's care. She begged me to find them and bring them to her in the throne realm, where they could negotiate their terms without violence. And she wanted me to take Maalik as backup. Of course, that wasn't happening, especially after he confessed to killing my mentor. The fact that it had been an order didn't make me hate him any less for it.

Before I could coin off to take care of business on my own, Grim ripped open the sky to the throne realm and began slaughtering original believers and devouring their soul matter. Naledi and I barely escaped with one other—Morgan, an original believer of the Fae.

After taking them to safety, I hurried to the mortal side, where Tasha Henry had made contact with one of Vince's souls. I followed him back to Vince's hideout where I was caught and tied up for interrogation. Before I could persuade Vince to meet with Naledi, Grim struck again.

I was bound and gagged in an office loft above the warehouse, where Vince had gathered the souls—safe but useless as I listened to the massacre happening downstairs.

Thankfully, Bub found me after Grim had left to rain his terror elsewhere. We discovered that *elsewhere* when we returned to Limbo and encountered a cyclone in the city park. It spiraled above Saul's and Coreen's memorial statues, spewing forth from a rift in the sky that matched the one in the throne realm.

Grim was soon at the center of it, drunk on soul matter and crushing the life from anyone who came within his reach—Jenni, Kevin, Gabriel, my hounds, Maalik.

Bub. I could do nothing to stop him. Until Naledi carved an opening by offering herself up to the demented god.

While she'd stripped my ability to see a soul's aura, the other gift I shared with Grim remained. She'd said that I still needed it. And at that moment, I knew why.

As Grim sucked the soul matter from her, I slipped behind him. By the time he noticed me, it was too late. I plunged my hands into his chest. But instead of pulling him out of existence, I absorbed the soul matter he'd stolen, taking it into myself until my head was so full of voices, I nearly forgot who *I* was.

With my last sliver of focus, I used the potent energy to resurrect those slain in the park. Then Naledi's voice led me to the Sea of Eternity, directing me to surrender the soul matter into the ghostly waters, along with the throne's spiritual bond to the mortal side.

A short distance off the coast, a series of small islands rose in response. Then, several souls gained corporeal consciousness and crawled ashore, celebrating their liberation from the sea. There was finally an afterlife for the faithless do-gooders. Ironic, maybe, but it was a beautiful sight, nonetheless. One that came with an epiphany.

This was my life's purpose. And it was complete.

Of course, the gods still bicker. There's just less to fight over these days, now that the Throne of Eternity is broken, and the excess soul matter flows into the sea.

But the Afterlife Council isn't my problem anymore.

I'm just a freelance soul harvester with *two* apprentices.

Right before Grim's last stand, the council approved that new generation of reapers Jenni had been after, and Naledi whipped them up lickety-split. Good thing, too. Without the excess soul matter or a soul on the throne, no new reapers could be created in the future.

This was it—the end of the line for our kind.

Not quite the way of the dodo or anything. I mean, we are immortal, after all.

But something about it felt so… final. As if we were hitting some collective, cosmic puberty—or leveling up.

Either way, ten years passed without much in the way of blood or tears. Harvesting souls was a less grim ordeal with the new afterlife on the Isles of Eternity. I managed to keep my apprentices and hellhounds alive, and I savored the good life with my demon in the Greek hell.

I no longer questioned my existence because my destiny had been fulfilled.

I never considered that I might have more than one.

CHAPTER ONE

*"I had a friend who was a clown. When he died,
all his friends went to the funeral in one car."*
—Steven Wright

TIME WORKED DIFFERENTLY between the mortal side
and Eternity. That was how Kevin, Eliza, and I were able
to coin off from the Limbo City harbor in full daylight
and end up in the pitch-black night on Coney Island.
Thankfully, reapers didn't suffer from jet lag.

Eliza folded her hands behind her head and reclined
on the roof of the Ferris wheel gondola. The stars spar-
kled in her eyes, and her breath fogged the crisp winter
air. Kevin stretched out beside her, chin propped in the
palm of one hand. His gaze darted from his watch to the
deserted amusement park below, where our marks
would be arriving any moment.

A handful of security lights lined the chain-link fence
that enclosed the park, separating it from the beach to
the south and Brooklyn to the north. The candy-striped
rides and coasters were quiet in the off-season. There

was no crowd to navigate, no potential doppelgangers to complicate our assignment. I expected this harvest to be a cakewalk despite its medium-risk status on my docket. Which was why I'd caved when Eliza had asked for a better view as we waited.

The moonless night melted into the ocean, blurring the horizon. I pulled the hood of my robe tighter around my neck and squinted, trying to find where the stars in the sky ended and their reflected twins began. They danced across the water as the waves kissed the shore.

Moments like these made the mortal realm seem almost tolerable.

I dangled my legs over the edge of the gondola roof and sighed. "Sure is a beautiful night."

"To die," Kevin added with a morbid, horror-film cackle.

As if on cue, a bloodcurdling scream tore through the park. My pulse quickened at the promise of death, but I held up a hand, signaling my apprentices to stay put. We already had the best seat in the house.

A second later, another scream bubbled up from the shadows, clearer this time. Then, a woman stumbled across a halo cast by one of the security lights.

Usually, I scoffed at the clumsy damsels who couldn't seem to stay on their feet while fleeing slasher-film killers. But then again, none of them had been in shoes ten sizes too big. The technicolor wig and obscene amount of makeup running down the woman's face finally pulled the full picture together.

"A clown?" Eliza hitched an eyebrow. "That's a first."

"Not for me. I scored a French mime in the 1840s," I boasted.

"Didn't you run a solo circus harvest back when we were with the Posy Unit?" Kevin asked, his eyes glued to the shadows, searching for our sad clown's pursuer.

"Yeah, but all the clowns made it out alive. And it wasn't *supposed* to be a solo harvest." I pressed my lips together, deciding not to dig up the past. Kevin had been clean for a decade, and he hadn't missed a single day of work in all that time.

"You said we're picking up three here. Right, boss?" Eliza asked, shifting focus back to our current assignment.

"Yup." I glanced at my watch. "One might already be dead, but he should be nearby. We'll collect him after the show."

"Oh, goody." Kevin rubbed his hands together and scooted closer to the edge. Eliza rolled her eyes, though she sat upright to get a better look for herself.

I was curious, too. The clown had surprised me. The profiles on my docket stuck to the basics unless a harvest was high-risk. I knew that all three souls we were picking up tonight worked their nine-to-fives as telemarketers at the same company, selling extended warranties. But I didn't know the specifics of their side hustles or hobbies. Apparently, clowning around was also something they had in common.

I saw the bloody knife before our killer, confirming my theory about the first victim. Then the light hit her pancake makeup, the stark white punctuated by black brows, rosy cheeks, and red geisha lips. Blood splattered her lavender leotard and matching tutu, and she stalked rather elegantly after her blubbering prey, balancing on the toes of her ballet slippers.

"Please!" the crying clown begged, tripping over her floppy shoes again. "I didn't know. He said you'd broken up!"

The killer clown slashed her knife through the air. She was too far away to do any damage, but the other woman screamed and tore off, heading for the Ferris wheel and forcing us to lean farther over the edge to catch the next act.

"Should we… move?" Eliza whispered.

"There." I nodded to the rooftop of a nearby attraction. "The spooky one with all the skeletons."

We rolled our coins and reappeared in time to watch the clowns begin their ascent up one of the Ferris wheel's support legs, awkwardly scaling the open-lattice metalwork. Neither of them wore the proper shoes for such an activity, but the ballerina seemed to be having an easier go of it.

"Man! I wish we had some popcorn." Kevin huffed and climbed up the backside of a skeletal dragon perched above the entrance of the building we'd moved to. Eliza snorted but craned her neck to watch as the clowns neared the center of the wheel, their limbs hooked hazardously over metal beams, panting breaths fogging between their faces.

The ballerina took another swipe with the butcher knife, this time making contact with the sad clown's forearm, drawing an earsplitting squeal from her. It was an overzealous strike, and the ballerina wobbled on her feet from the momentum. She grasped for the nearest beam, letting the knife slip from her hand. It clattered between the rungs before freefalling to the pavement below.

"You crazy bitch!" the sad clown screamed, clutching her bleeding arm to her chest. She was suddenly braver now that the knife was out of play. "No wonder Ron was afraid to dump you!"

Not to be discouraged, the ballerina clown braced her back against a beam and reached into the sleeve of her leotard, retrieving a silk handkerchief—or twenty. They were knotted together, likely for a less nefarious purpose than strangling her cheating ex's side piece.

She waited for her flopsy-footed quarry to begin down the metal lattice. The knife was on the ground, and

I saw the hopeful glint in the sad clown's eyes. She thought there was a chance she could reach it first and survive this.

But as soon as she was a rung below the ballerina, the colorful noose slipped over her head. Flopsy garbled out a strangled cry and clawed at her neck, releasing her hold on the base of the Ferris wheel. Her oversized shoes wobbled on the beam she was perched on, just barely keeping her upright.

Eliza sucked in a sharp breath and covered her eyes, immediately peeking through her fingers. I stifled a smirk. There was no escaping the morbid curiosity that came with being a reaper. It was in our blood.

A hollow, scraping sound drew my gaze back to the Ferris wheel. Flopsy's giant shoes had finally failed her. She kicked at the metal beams, trying to regain her footing. But it was too late. The ballerina released the rope.

The sad clown's skull bounced off a crossbeam on the way down, concussing her enough that she didn't even muster a scream before her body smacked the pavement and began the telltale oozing of a violent death.

"Is the ballerina butcher our third?" Kevin whispered. "Or is there another victim hiding around here somewhere?" He was entirely too eager.

I huffed. "Do you really want me to spoil the surprise?"

Okay, so maybe I wasn't exactly discouraging this behavior. But was loving your job such a bad thing? Besides, these extra colorful harvests were a rare treat.

"No, don't tell us," Eliza said, now fully invested in the final act.

Sirens echoed in the distance. A second later, red and blue lights flickered across Brooklyn's dark skyline.

I turned back to the Ferris wheel, waiting to see how our murderous ballerina would react. I expected surprise or panic. Maybe some nervous fumbling. But she remained calm, graceful even, as she slipped down one of the diagonal rungs. It was as if she were following the steps of a choreographed dance, performing a show for the ghosts of her victims—or us.

And then the toe of her slipper found the spot where the sad clown's split skull had bloodied the beam, making it slick. Much too slick for her murderous victory pirouettes.

Even her swan song was elegant. It wailed in harmony with the approaching sirens, cutting off sharply as she met her end in a pile of skewed limbs beside the sad clown.

"Aww," Kevin groaned. "That was a cheap finale. Not even a shootout with the fuzz?"

I shook my head. "Clearly, I've been giving you too many gangster harvests."

"I thought it was poetic justice," Eliza said. "And I can't wait to question their souls. This should be good." She hiked up her robe to retrieve the retractable scythe holstered on her hip.

Reapers Inc. had contracted Warren, armorer to the Nephilim Guard, to design a few harvesting gadgets. Since we were personal friends, that meant my team and I got to test drive said gadgets—for better or worse.

The retractable scythe was his latest creation. Unfortunately, mine had been useless since last Tuesday, after I'd gotten the business end stuck in the eye of a hellcat. In *Chicago*.

The creatures had been appearing more frequently on the mortal side, but no one could figure out where they were coming from. Was there a rift in the soul matter that separated one side of the grave from the other? Or perhaps a new old god with a bone to pick now that the Throne of Eternity had been dissolved, and an infinitely powerful soul no longer lingered in the shadows like Grim's invisible watchdog?

It wasn't really my place anymore to seek out the answers to those questions—even if it *did* make my job more problematic. That was Afterlife Council business, and I was more than happy to stay off their radar these days. I just wished their problems would stay off *my* radar.

In the meantime, I needed a tune-up on my retractable scythe. I still preferred my battle axe when it came to most high-risk assignments, but until the hellcat issue was resolved, I required something more practical to get me through the workday in one piece.

"I'll go track down the first soul," Kevin offered, shouting over the nearing sirens. I nodded and pointed Eliza at the two clowns under the Ferris wheel.

"Let's get this show on the road before they turn into chalk outlines."

CHAPTER TWO

"When I was a boy, the Dead Sea was only sick."
—*George Burns*

Even though I now resided in Tartarus with Beelzebub, it was hard not to think of Limbo as home. I'd spent three hundred years in the city, and even its flaws had a certain charm. The ancient, rickety dock piers that were constantly being repaired. The nosy goddess shopkeepers. The faerie-inhabited woods scattered along the coast.

These were the devils I knew, unlike the occasional raining fire and brimstone smog that rolled in off the Styx near the manor in Tartarus. The gritty, yellow aftermath stained the windows and clung to my hellhounds' fur like tar that stank of rotten eggs. I wasn't sure I'd ever get used to that—or the professional grooming bills that came as a result.

But it wasn't as if I could just pick up and move back to Limbo City. Not unless I wanted to live on my ship in the harbor with my apprentices. Holly Spirit, my last landlord, would have been a terrible reference, even if my hounds hadn't left their *special* mark on my former condo at Holly House.

Ah, well. Thumbing my nose at that holier-than-thou twat had been worth the pricey commute. And I still enjoyed an occasional night out at Purgatory Lounge or a shopping excursion with Ellen. Of course, it had been several months since I'd last seen Grim's former secretary. I could accept half the blame for that.

Ellen hated harvesting souls. It was an acquired taste, and she had a millennium of experience in an entirely different occupation that she *had* enjoyed. I wasn't the one who had vasectomized the Throne of Eternity and put an end to the centennial addition of new reapers. Still, Ellen accused me of being the catalyst for Grim going off the deep end—which was fair—and thus considered me the responsible party for her unsavory situation—which was totally *not* fair.

Whenever we spent time together, the conversation always found its way around to my ties with Jenni Fang. When had I last spoken to her? Did she seem overwhelmed with paperwork? Was her coffee mug full?

I didn't have the heart to tell Ellen that Regina, the nephilim who had replaced her at the front desk, was working out just fine. I'd had my reservations about the winged newbie during her first few months, but aside from a handful of docket mix-ups, she'd managed to keep things in order at Reapers Inc. for the past decade. She'd even collaborated with Warren and the Fates on a new digital docket system.

The tablet interface required serious security measures with facial recognition and duress lock-out codes. Though I was most interested in the features that allowed me to shave half an hour off the workday. The instant data transfer meant daily visits to the office were no longer necessary.

Unfortunately, Warren couldn't fix my busted scythe without an in-person visit.

I shucked my work robe and parted ways with Kevin and Eliza at the harbor, leaving them to deliver the day's catch without me. Coin travel had been deactivated within the city, and with no throne soul, there was no way to change that. The travel booths were still operational, but I opted to save my money and walk.

I skipped the busy historic district down Morte Avenue and took Council Street instead. As I neared the park, my gaze drew up, taking in a pale crease slashed across the sky. The white lines spiderwebbed over a smear of lilac, marring the deeper evening blue. It looked like crinkled paper, or maybe a wispy tangle of clouds.

For how little things had changed in Eternity once the throne was broken, the realm where Naledi and her Apparition Agency once lived had begun decomposing almost immediately. The gaping hole Grim had ripped in the sky wasn't so much healing as it was collapsing.

The pocket realm was disappearing—fading from existence. The travel booths no longer accepted it as a destination either. Gabriel and Maalik had attempted to enter from above, but there'd been nothing to see. No ground to land upon. Ten years later, this faded crease in the sky was all that remained of the throne realm.

Nostalgia stabbed at my heart as my gaze dropped to the bronze statues and marble bench in the park. Visiting the memorials always drenched me in melancholy, but it also reminded me how lucky I was. Not just to be alive, but to have had Saul and Josie—and even Coreen—in my life.

I shoved my hands into the pockets of my leather jacket and headed down Council Street, vowing to return for a proper visit soon. Maybe I'd drag Kevin and Gabriel along. Or take the hounds for a run around the city to enjoy the cooler air and clear my lungs of brimstone. I put my Limbo City daydreaming on hold as I neared the entrance to Reapers Inc.

Warren still lived at Holly House, but he'd moved his workshop to the seventy-first floor of the Reapers Inc. building, one level above the Nephilim Guard station, which happened to be two floors below the Afterlife Council headquarters. Run-ins with council members never seemed to go well for me, so I avoided them whenever possible—with the exception of Meng Po, whom I visited at least once a month for tea with her, Jai Ling, and Jack.

A pair of reapers pushed through the double doors, and I jerked to a stop, my heart lurching at the thought of bumping into Holly, Cindy, Ridwan, or Maalik. I wished like hell I had Morgan's invisibility necklace on me, but that would have been a cowardly misuse of the relic. Not to mention the questions it would raise if the security footage were reviewed. I didn't need to give the council a reason to take anything else away from me.

I sucked in a deep breath and darted inside the building, avoiding eye contact with anyone on my way to the elevators. I lucked out and slipped in with a pair of nephilim as the doors to their lift began sliding shut.

"Seventy-fifth floor?" the taller of the two asked, his wings shuddering as he gave me a once-over, taking in the dark hair and pale complexion that marked me as a reaper.

"Seventy-first, please." I patted the sheath fastened to my hip, making sure it was still there.

The nephilim nodded and pressed the button for the correct floor. The sixty-ninth was already lit on the panel, which could only mean they were new trainees for the Guard.

Jenni Fang's solution to the hellcats plaguing the mortal side had been to send the Nephilim Guard out to investigate and round up any strays reported during harvests. The problem had become so severe that the latest digital docket upgrade included an automatic incident report feature, but the extra detail was spreading the Guard too thin. They'd had to up their recruiting efforts and offer sign-on bonuses.

The elevator paused to let its feathered passengers off before continuing upward, and I heaved a sigh of relief when it reached my destination without stopping to collect anyone new. Part of me resented the anxiety I managed to carry around all these years later. I feared I would always be making a conscious effort to stay out of everyone's way in this city—no matter my accomplishments. It couldn't be helped.

"Well, well, well," Warren greeted me in the lobby of his armory. A blacksmith apron hung around his neck, protecting the green plaid flannel and khakis he wore beneath. "We meet again, my old foe," he said in a playful, craggy voice. "What have you broken this time?"

"It wasn't my fault. The hellcat was extra feisty," I explained as I unhooked the sheathed scythe. Warren heaved an annoyed sigh and accepted it from me.

"These were supposed to be for emergencies only. To keep unruly souls in line. Their design is more for show than battle."

"It *was* an emergency!" I insisted. "I could have lost a soul."

"Lana." He pressed his lips together. "This is like, the *tenth* one you've either broken or lost."

"That last one was defective." My chest puffed out, and I jabbed a finger at my face. "It nearly put my eye out!"

"That's because you tried to fold it up with a mangled blade."

"I've worked with butterknives more durable."

Warren bristled and turned away from me. "You're lucky I like you." He pressed the telescoping button on the holster that doubled as the scythe's grip once it extended. The shaft unfolded as expected, clicking softly as each piece aligned with the last. Until it reached the very end.

The hooked blade was thin and flexible. It had to be so it could fit inside the cylindrical sheath. And though it was sharper than hell, it was flimsy. As made evident by how the blade at the end of mine dangled haphazardly, creaking out a pitiful tale of abuse.

"The hinge is busted," Warren snapped. "What'd you do, step on it again?"

"No." I flushed, recalling my first mishap with the gadget. "I told you, there was a hellcat. The blade got stuck behind the beast's eye socket."

"Uh-huh." Warren sighed and fingered the loose joint that required repair. "I'll have Lindy fix this up by Friday. Can I trust you with a loaner in the meantime?"

"Of course." I gave him a tight smile that he returned with a grimace.

"Yup," he said, wings twitching. "You're *so* lucky I like you."

"I am, aren't I?"

"Come on, then." Warren waved his free arm, directing me to follow him down a side hallway off the lobby. He had no front desk or secretary, but he *did* have three employees to help make and repair his weapons and gadgets now.

If ever there were a rags-to-riches story among Warren's kind, it was his. His arsenal continued to evolve in leaps and bounds, from a trunk that had served as his coffee table in a rundown basement apartment to a spare bedroom in his condo at Holly House, and now to an entire floor in a skyscraper.

I couldn't help but feel a twinge of pride for having played a part in his rise to fame and fortune. Even with all the grief I'd caused Warren since, I knew he still held me in high esteem. *Clearly*, if he were willing to loan me a scythe after the way mine looked.

"How's the soul gauntlet litigation going?" I asked as we curled around a corner and paused at a locked door. Warren groaned. It was a touchy subject, but I was curious.

"The Afterlife Council declined the latest model. Now, they want me to integrate it with the digital dockets so the cuff will only accept approved souls. They're worried about the damage a soul poacher might do if they get ahold of one."

"Sure they are." I scoffed. The Afterlife Council had too much time on their hands with no throne or soul matter to squabble over. Therefore, they had to find other ways to validate their position and pay—even if that was just being a pain in everyone else's ass. It seemed those closest to me had suffered the most—like Warren. But he wasn't letting it slow him down much.

He pressed his hand to a screen beside the door we'd stopped at and leaned forward so a laser on a second panel could scan his eyes. It felt like overkill, but he *was* harboring quite a lethal collection.

"Passcode," a computerized voice demanded.

"Hairy cherub," Warren answered. A second later, the lock released, and the door popped open.

I snorted. "Some password."

"It's not, actually." Warren grinned. "I can say anything I like. The computer is simply measuring the pitch and tone of my voice to determine if I'm being coerced."

"Fancy."

"The door will still open, mind you. For five seconds. Then, it will lock again, trapping anyone inside and alerting the Guard."

I gave the threshold a cautious glance as I followed him inside the room, hoping the system hadn't detected the anxiety my heavy-handedness had surely caused Warren. I was glad he hadn't entered his techno-security phase until *after* I'd helped Tasha Henry escape. I was sure they were making good use of Warren's new skillset at the Nephilim Guard headquarters, too.

The black interior of the room muted the overhead lights. Square shelves filled with scythe sheaths and loose shaft pieces outlined blade-laden pegboards. The opposite wall held bins of hardware and tools for assembly, and a narrow stack of shelves on the far wall held the finished products.

Warren deposited my busted weapon on a stainless-steel table that stretched the length of the room and fetched a new scythe before turning back to me. "Here we go," he said, pulling it out of my reach as I grasped for it. "Take it easy on this one, yeah?"

"Oh, for sure." I squeaked out a nervous laugh, and he reluctantly handed over the scythe. I was extra delicate while fastening it to my belt. "See? Safe and sound."

"Uh-huh." Warren's shoulders sagged. He might like me, but that didn't mean he was confident in my ability not to break his precious creations.

"It's only for a few days, right?" I offered, trying to soothe his concern. "I probably won't even need to use it."

"Uh-huh." A feather shook loose from one of his wings. Great, he was already molting on me.

We retraced our steps to the lobby, where I thanked him again before pressing the button for an elevator. I was ready to get out of there and head back to the harbor where I could coin home and share a bottle of wine with my demon.

And I would have done just that, if Jenni Fang hadn't been waiting for me when the elevator doors slid open.

CHAPTER THREE

*"There is something about a closet
that makes a skeleton terribly restless."*
—*Wilson Mizner*

MAYBE I HAD IMAGINED IT, but I thought that Jenni
Fang and I had been on the verge of friendship at one time.
Our differences were many, but we'd found balance in our
common denominator: Josie Galla.

If not for Josie, I didn't imagine Jenni and I would have
ever been roommates or study buddies or gone shopping together. The only time Jenni had involved me without Josie
present had been when Grim approved her revenge mission
on Caim.

After he'd taken Jenni, I'd been the one to find her, albeit
naked and chained in a dark cell, broken both mentally and
physically. I'd assumed she'd chosen me to go after Caim because she knew I'd understand her wrath and desperate need
for closure. Not exactly a girls' night out, but battle was its
own flavor of bonding.

A part of me had always suspected that Jenni knew
more than she'd let on after becoming Grim's new

second-in-command. Not that I imagined Grim had shared the information freely, but Jenni was resourceful. And ambitious. A combination that made her too much like our late boss for my taste. The slick black pantsuits she'd taken to wearing only amplified the similarity.

Jenni leaned against the elevator's back wall, ankles crossed and arms folded. "Going down?" she asked at my slack-jawed hesitation.

"Uh… yeah." I gave Warren a farewell nod and boarded the elevator with an uneasy feeling in my gut.

Jenni's complete lack of surprise made it clear that our meeting this way was not a coincidence. As soon as the doors closed, she pressed the button for the thirty-seventh floor. My stomach clenched, even though it had been years since I'd last visited Grim's floor of horrors, reserved for torturing his foes.

"It's been a long day," Jenni said, her stoic gaze briefly meeting mine. "Have a drink with me."

"You know, I would, but Bub's expecting me for dinner, and um…" I raked a hand through my hair, trying to summon a better excuse.

Jenni shot me another look, one that reminded me far too much of Grim. "I wasn't asking."

I wheezed out a clipped laugh. "Sounds as if I'm going to *need* that drink."

"You and me both."

"How did you even know I was here?" I asked, my senses finally catching up.

"Tracking chip in your soul docket."

My hand instinctively went to my pocket, patting the outline of the device through my pants. It wasn't much bigger than a cell phone, making it easy to forget after the workday ended. But I wouldn't forget it again. That sucker would be staying on the ship anytime I was off the clock from here on out.

I wasn't the sort to engage in illegal activities—well, not anymore. It was the principal of the matter. That kind of invasive technology should be reserved for emergencies, not used to ambush me in an elevator. I didn't enjoy being caught off guard. I didn't know anyone who did.

"How do you like your martinis?" Jenni asked as the elevator rolled to a stop.

"At home," I muttered under my breath.

"Gin or vodka?" she clarified, ignoring my snarky nerves.

Before I could answer, the doors slid open, revealing a bright foyer.

The construction site I remembered with its hanging plastic sheets and abandoned power tools was gone. A giant marble geisha squatted in one corner, her head nearly grazing the high ceiling. She clutched a bucket in her hands, tilted so that it continuously spilled into a raised basin at her feet. Fat koi splashed their tails in greeting as Jenni sat on the lip of the fountain. She twirled her fingers in the water and then took off her heels, exchanging them for a pair of house slippers.

The elevator doors began to close again, and I slapped my hand out to stop them, quickly exiting at Jenni's irritated scowl. She pointed toward a bench along the far wall. "You can kick your boots off over there."

I did as instructed and then followed her down a curved hallway and into a massive living space. Evening light filtered through tall windows. The sky had melted into a deep red-orange, painting the walls and cabinets a golden hue.

Jenni cut through the room, bypassing a pristine sitting area. The absence of throw pillows and ass impressions in the angular, leather sofas made it clear the room didn't get much use.

"Do you... *live* here?" I was almost embarrassed that I didn't know the answer. Had we really become so out of touch?

"For two years now," Jenni answered. She stopped in front of a wet bar and filled a shaker with ice before pulling two martini glasses from a glass chiller. "Gin or vodka?" she asked again.

"Gin, thanks." I stripped out of my jacket and glanced around the room, trying to decide where to discard it. Now that I was reasonably certain that Jenni hadn't gone full-on sadist and brought me here to witness her grim handiwork, my heart rate had returned to normal. Maybe we really could just be two old friends sharing a drink after work.

"You can toss that anywhere," Jenni said, nodding at the catalog-worthy sitting area.

I draped my jacket over the back of a sofa and cringed at how it ruined the aesthetic. I didn't belong in perfect places like this. I was a messy, lived-in kinda gal. An overstuffed chaise covered in knit blankets and hellhound fur was more my speed.

Jenni carried our martinis to a long counter that sectioned off the kitchen and pulled out a pair of backless barstools that had been pushed up against the paneled underside. Their leather seats matched the sofas and looked as equally unused as everything else in the apartment. I couldn't decide if it was because Jenni was just that anal or if she stayed too busy to entertain.

"Two years?" I hitched an eyebrow and gave the place an appraising glance before taking a seat.

"The condo at Holly House wasn't getting much use, and then the council began to question the conflict of interest." Jenni rolled her eyes and took a sip of her martini.

I plucked up the cocktail sword of olives in my glass, biting one off to keep my mouth busy. Jenni already knew how I felt about the council, and *everyone* knew how desperate they were to appear relevant in the changing political landscape of Eternity. Nitpicking the president of Reapers Inc.'s living accommodations made about as much sense as anything else they'd done in the past decade.

I finally sampled the martini, washing down the olive with an appreciative hum. The gin was smooth with an herbal aftertaste. It steeled my nerves just enough to get me into trouble. "You never track me down to have drinks. What's the occasion?"

"Right to it, then." Jenni polished off her martini and set it on the counter, swallowing hard before her gaze locked on mine again. "We have a problem, and I think you're the only one who can solve it."

"And by *we*, you mean... the council?"

"No." Jenni shook her head. "I mean *we* as in all of Eternity. Everyone."

I huffed and propped an elbow on the edge of the counter. "Look, I know they'd love to get their hands on an original believer who's willing to restore the throne. But even if I wanted to help them—which I *don't*—they stripped me of the ability to see a soul's aura. So, I don't see how I could possibly be a better candidate than anyone else for whatever problem—"

"When's the last time you talked to Ellen Aries?" Jenni asked, her expression going stony.

"I don't know. A few months ago?" I shrugged.

"Do you remember shadowing her when she first reentered the field?"

"Sure." A cold sweat worked its way up my back to the nape of my neck. "Why?"

"That was after Naledi's procedure."

"And?" I blinked innocently.

Jenni's eyes narrowed. By now, I knew where she was going with this, but I still held out hope that I might be able to bullshit my way out of it.

"Ellen claims that a soul could see you *perimortem*."

"What? When?"

"The hospital where you encountered Vince Hare." Jenni laced her fingers together in her lap. "I assume that was an original believer. Maybe that's why Vince was interested in him? It's possible he had a seer in his little cult of souls."

"I honestly don't know." I pinched my eyes closed as unwelcome memories of what had followed flooded my mind. "Grim killed him, along with Vince and everyone else he recruited."

"That doesn't change the fact that he was able to see you before his death," Jenni said.

"The guy was losing his mind. He was screaming for more dessert. That doesn't prove he could see me."

"It's going to take a lot more than that to convince the council."

"Why does the council have to know about this at all?" I snapped. "It's useless information that serves no purpose. I won't help rebuild the corrupt system I was born to dismantle—" I jumped as Jenni's hand slapped the countertop, cutting me off.

"You weren't born—you were made. Just like the rest of us," she said through clenched teeth. "And if I don't share this information with the council at tomorrow's meeting, Ms. Aries has advised me that the captain of the Guard intends to."

Ellen had sold me out. The cold sweat on my neck suddenly felt hot.

"It doesn't matter." I lifted my chin. "Even if that soul *did* see me, I haven't come across another who could since. I'm useless to the council, and that's exactly how I'd like to remain."

"Lana." Jenni dragged a hand down her face. "This isn't just about taking control of the excess soul matter. The boundaries of the hells are shifting unpredictably. The hellcat and rogue demon sightings on the mortal side are becoming more and more frequent, and Ross's troops are the ones suffering for it. In his position, who wouldn't do everything in their power to solve this crisis?"

"And how do the souls on the Isles of Eternity feel about *solving* this crisis?" I countered. "Do you really think they're going to give up their territory and autonomy so easily?"

Jenni shook her head. "No one is asking them to. The council isn't even interested in the throne right now. They think original believers could be useful in other ways."

"Sure they do." I held my hands out, palms up. "It doesn't really matter, though. Like I said, I haven't come across another original believer."

"Yes, but we haven't been actively searching for them, have we?"

"Great." I groaned and downed the rest of my martini. The idea of going in front of the council again made my nerves twitch. Maybe I could avoid that if I sucked it up and agreed to this now. "I take it the Special Ops Unit will be reinstated?"

"That's what I'm recommending to the council in the morning." Jenni stood and collected our empty glasses. "Do you want another?"

"That depends. Do you have any more nasty surprises to spring on me?"

"Not at the moment."

"Then I'll pass."

Jenni set my glass in the wet bar sink and fixed herself a second cocktail as the golden light in the apartment shifted to a dusty violet. The empty walls and pale floors soaked up the color. The thirty-seventh floor was high enough above the city to allow a view of the Sea of Eternity in the distance.

Just past the harbor, the largest of the Isles of Eternity bloomed with a dark forest, enclosing the private community of souls within its protective wall of evergreens. They'd established their own rules early on, and no outsiders were allowed to set foot on their territory.

Jenni had tried to foster goodwill by offering the new souls work visas for Limbo City. With so much of the nephilim population joining the Guard, the workforce could have used the boost. The souls had declined, though they had elected an ambassador to join the council. The council had reluctantly agreed to the addition since it was their only way of gathering information about the new territory they'd just as soon sink back into the sea.

Despite never having visited the islands or the souls that inhabited them, I couldn't help but feel a certain level of responsibility for their existence. Sure, the throne's power had ultimately created them—but I'd been the one to unleash it into the sea. That had to count for something.

Not that I'd ever tried to lay claim to the territory. What was I going to do with a bunch of undeveloped islands? And who needed the extra pain in the ass with the council and their constant plotting? No thank you.

Besides, I was genuinely happy for the souls the throne had deemed worthy of an afterlife.

I should have known I'd be the one expected to take it from them.

CHAPTER FOUR

*"No one is actually dead until the ripples
they cause in the world die away."*
—*Terry Pratchett*

It WAS LATE, AND I KNEW Bub would worry if I didn't make it home soon, but I stopped at the park anyway. Talking to Saul's memorial statue or Josie's marble bench always proved therapeutic, and I needed a moment to pull myself together before dumping this latest news on my significant demon.

What I didn't need was a broody angel of Allah cramping my style.

"I thought you might drop by," Maalik said, his back still turned to me as he stared up at the bronze likeness of my late mentor. Silvery wings lay folded against his black robe, his waterfall of inky curls nestled between their swells. "Please, don't go," he added as I glanced over my shoulder, shooting an anxious look back toward the street.

"I didn't come here to see *you*," I said, not caring how callous I sounded.

The last kindness I'd afforded Maalik had been resurrecting him with the power of the throne before giving it over to the sea. If I'd been in my right mind, I wasn't so sure I would have. A few hours before Grim's soul-sucking standoff, Maalik had confessed to killing Saul Avelo.

Living in Tartarus meant minimal chance of bumping into Maalik. I appreciated the buffer, and not just because I could hardly stand the sight of him. Learning what he'd done to my mentor had activated the most wrathful power I shared with Grim. It bubbled hot beneath the surface, daring me to dismantle Maalik's soul matter and scatter it to the night sky.

The ability was even more concerning and unpredictable than whatever lingering, reverse soul vision I had going on. It had destroyed even the memory of Craig Hogan while leaving Grim's known history untouched. If I had to guess, it was because Grim's origin had been rooted in a mortal belief structure, while Craig had simply been fashioned from raw soul matter. Naledi would have known for certain, but she was gone, too. There was no one I could go to for answers about these so-called gifts or why I still had them.

"President Fang and I discussed her meeting with Ms. Aries this afternoon," Maalik said, finally turning to face me. "I was hardly surprised to learn that you'd re-tained some of the abilities Khadija bestowed upon you."

"Why would Jenni tell you before the rest of the council?"

"She asked that I support her proposal to reinstate the Special Ops Unit."

"And, what? You thought you'd be first in line to barter a vote for a favor?" I folded my arms, tucking my hands out of sight for fear they might start glowing. "Well, joke's on you. No one is blackmailing me this time, so I have zero interest in the unit. I won't be hand-ing out any favors for the privilege of running it."

"I don't want a favor—I mean, I do, but…" Maalik's wings twitched as he struggled to find his next words. "You have my endorsement regardless, of course. That's not what I intended to barter."

"Then, what?" I blinked at him. "What could you possibly have that you think I would ever, in a million years, want?"

"It's not what *I* have." He licked the corner of his mouth and stole a nervous glance around the park as the wind kicked up, rattling the last of fall's dead leaves across the sidewalk. "Khadija is willing to pay triple the council's base bid if you give the soul candidate for Ja-hannam top priority."

My breath caught. "Khadija?"

It was hard to think of the original throne soul as the same person after she'd drunk Meng's tea and forgot the role she'd played in shaping Eternity. In shaping *me*. But hearing her name still made my heart stutter.

"Wait…" I glared at Maalik. "What do you mean *candidate* for Jahannam? The council doesn't actually intend to use a hell-bound soul to restore the throne, do they? Have you all lost your damn minds?"

"Certainly not." Maalik's shoulders squared at the accusation. "This soul's purpose would be to stabilize Jahannam's boundaries."

Jenni had said the council thought original believers could be useful in other ways, but I remained skeptical. I didn't know how Khadija had used her power to create the throne. And after Meng Po's mindwipe tea, I supposed she didn't remember how she'd done it either.

It was for the best. No single soul or deity deserved to have that kind of power over all of Eternity.

But, if the council *were* trying to restore the throne, collecting original believers to experiment with would be the first step. Ordering me to track down potential candidates was one thing. Requesting malevolent souls was quite another.

As much as I despised Maalik, he was a righteous asshole. He wouldn't be compelled to do anything to the detriment of Eternity. And though he hadn't openly confessed that he'd offed Saul, he hadn't lied to my face about it after I found out either.

I narrowed my gaze on the angel. "When the rest of the council learns that I might, *might* still be able to identify original believers, do you honestly think they won't try to use me to find a soul to restore the throne?"

To Maalik's credit, he didn't break eye contact when he answered. "I don't pretend to know the ulterior motives of anyone but myself."

"Well, that's convenient."

"It's the truth," he countered. "But if we're playing a guessing game, then yes, I suppose it is possible that one or more members of the council will see this development as a means to restore the throne. Though it will be quite some time before they agree on a worthy soul for the job, so you need not worry about that now. We have more pressing matters at hand."

The park lights flickered on, including the beacon held high in the hand of Coreen's memorial statue. It painted glowing outlines around everything, reminding me of the sparkling blue auras I'd once been able to see surrounding the most sacred souls. The thought left a bitter taste in my mouth.

Maalik's wings fluttered nervously at my silence. "The popular theory is that the unaffected realms are stable because they have resident original believers," he explained. "Heaven has Mary and Peter. Jannah has

Khadija. Summerland has the Pythia. Chitragupta keeps meticulous records, so Svarga and Naraka have been spared, as well."

"And Jahannam is without?"

"Among others." Maalik nodded. "The soul matter that holds the borders of the Islamic hell—between the other afterlives and the mortal realm—is weak. Khadija's presence maintains Jannah, but without another to stabilize Jahannam, it draws from her, as well. And she had precious little strength to spare after spending so long on the throne."

"If she's so weak, why isn't this offer coming from Muhammad?" I demanded, feeling indignant on Khadija's behalf.

"The prophet is on the Board of Heavenly Hosts. It's best not to involve him in this… unauthorized business."

"Unauthorized?" I smirked. The pained look on Maalik's face made me itch to gloat. The Angel of Hellfire and Law and Order was trying to broker an illegal transaction. The irony wasn't lost on either of us.

"Yes." He bit off the word. "This deal would be under the table, so to speak."

"I don't want Khadija's coin." I hated Maalik, but there would always be room for Khadija in my heart. "I owe her everything," I said, sincerity washing away my scorn. "If I have any say in the matter, of course I'll give Jahannam's soul priority."

"Take the money." Maalik's brow furrowed at my obvious confusion. "She won't understand your kindness, and explaining it to her would prove more complicated than I think you realize. She has no memory of her time on the throne. It would only upset her."

"Fine. Whatever." I unfolded my arms and turned to walk away.

"One last thing," he added, drawing my attention again. "While it is a generous offer, Khadija is willing to increase the amount if anyone else approaches you."

I frowned. "And who else might I expect an offer from?"

"Hard to say for certain." Maalik shrugged and let his gaze slide away. "I've heard rumors that the ghost market has reformed."

"You really think I would sell a soul on the ghost market?" Heat pulsed in my chest, and I inched back a step. I needed to get out of there before I went supernova.

"I think it's possible they may approach you once news spreads about the Special Ops Unit's comeback," Maalik said. "This is just a precaution."

"I'll keep that in mind." I dipped my chin in a curt nod and stalked off, not giving him a chance to say anything else.

Despite the winter chill settling in with the darkness of night, my blood needed distance to cool down, and he'd spoiled the sliver of peace I'd hoped to gain before heading home. But Maalik was good at that—I hadn't expected anything less from him. And now, even more weighed on my heart.

With hellcats loose on the mortal side, I could have guessed the problem lay with one or more of the hells. It was in their nature, the same way destroying my peace of mind was in Maalik's. But the question was, which other afterlives needed an original believer?

If a do-gooder angel were willing to offer me a bribe, I shuddered to think who else might soon seek me out. I guessed I should have been glad that I only had bribes to worry about this time and not blackmail. Not that it made my job any less tedious.

But I'd take money over death threats any day of the week.

CHAPTER FIVE

"Go to Heaven for the climate, Hell for the company."
—*Mark Twain*

My phone rang the second I stepped off the dock in Tartarus. There was still a soft puddle of light in the sky here, amber honey bleeding into a pink horizon. I breathed in the brimstone-tinged air and answered on the second ring.

"I'm outside," I said. "Heading in now."

"Come around back," Bub replied. "I'm elbow-deep in the corpse lilies."

"Joy." I suppressed a dismayed grumble and hung up.

Bub's indefinite sabbatical after being maimed by rebels during the Second War of Eternity had blossomed into a zealous obsession with gardening—hellscaping, as he called it. The garden of horrors in our backyard had taken on a life of its own, growing to more than three times the size the original garden had been before the fire.

I wanted to be happy that my demon had a hobby he was passionate about—one that kept him out of trouble with the bigwigs of the underworld, who only saw him as an expendable pawn. But mostly, I found myself tolerating the garden, especially the stinky plants that made our outdoor dining area all but useless. At least it offered a shady spot for my hellhounds to nap.

Saul and Coreen were stretched out under the table, their black fur dusted yellow from the most recent storm. They lifted their muzzles in unison, acknowledging me with soft snorts to let me know they were still put out over not being allowed inside the house.

I couldn't even bear to take them to work with me in their condition. They smelled like Gabriel's morning hangover farts. Standing downwind from them triggered my gag reflex. Of course, it was nothing compared to the corpse lilies Bub had taken a shine to recently.

The flowers were enormous, each of their rubbery, rust-colored petals larger than a serving tray. I'd thought them pretty, at first. Until I caught a whiff of the rotten corpse fragrance for which they'd been nicknamed.

Bub claimed the stench was to draw in the flies and beetles needed for pollination, but that only occurred if the insects first survived the pot-like center designed to trap and consume them. It was a more passive feast than that of the sunflower-flytrap hybrids Bub grew behind the corpse lilies to provide shade and feed the carnivorous plants more efficiently. The beetles and grasshoppers that escaped the taller flytraps fell into the corpse lilies' sticky pots.

Both plants would also feed on flies, but Bub's foot soldiers were too clever for that. They served as reliable, stealthy pollinators for the corpse lilies, a feat my demon boasted made him the first ever to breed these abominations in captivity. I was convinced that he was the first ever to *want* that distinction.

A stone wall bordered three sides of the garden, tapering into a wrought-iron fence that enclosed the side facing the back of the manor. It had been knocked down and rebuilt twice now to accommodate Bub's growing collection of nightmarish delights.

The pond in the center of the garden had grown, too. Less so for the water plants than for Ursula. Our pet octopus had long surpassed her species' average size. I was beginning to wonder if there'd been a tank mix-up at the pet shop. There was clearly Kraken DNA in her genome somewhere.

As I neared the garden, a pair of tentacles unfurled in greeting, and two button eyes broke the surface of the pond. It felt rude not to wave back, so I did, but I used my other hand to cover my nose and mouth before approaching Bub.

My demon was clad in dirty jeans and an unbuttoned flannel, the sleeves rolled up to his elbows. His dark hair hung past his shoulders, and he'd taken to tying back the top half. His beard had grown out, too, giving him a wild, rugged look that was growing on me.

"Long day at the office, love?" he asked, taking a step back from the raised flower bed where a few of his flies buzzed back and forth between the corpse lilies.

"Too long to endure much of this," I mumbled from behind my fingers, doing my best to breathe through my mouth. "Has Rupert started on dinner?" I glanced back toward the house, eager for an excuse to get away from the garden as soon as possible.

"I should hope so," Bub snarled even as he leaned in to give me a peck on the temple. "We're having eggplant parmesan. Let's hope he doesn't burn it this time."

"It wasn't that bad," I said, instinctively defending our newest butler.

"Really?" Bub scoffed. "Is that why you didn't clear your plate either?"

"I had too much garlic bread and salad—both of which were excellent."

"So?" Bub gave me a withering scowl. "What kind of wanker screws up a salad?"

Rupert was the latest in a long line of potential replacements that would never measure up to the standard of living Jack had provided. Not according to the Lord of the Flies, at least. But Jack had moved on, and we were trying to, as well.

Bub took my free hand and led me toward the shed beside the greenhouse nursery he'd built last summer. His wheelbarrow and a collection of gardening tools littered the ground. "I called Hades' Hound House this morning," he said, changing the subject as he gathered up a shovel and rake.

"Please tell me they're able to get our heathens in soon."

"First thing tomorrow. Also"—his grin tightened, and the corners of his eyes crinkled—"Persephone happened to be in the shop when I called. She and Hades have invited us to dinner tomorrow evening."

"Really?" I blinked at him. "That's a first."

"Yes, I was surprised, too. But she was insistent, claiming she and Hades never got to properly thank you for reclaiming the Cap of Invisibility."

"Oh." My stomach dropped at hearing that the invitation had been directed more toward me, and I was too slow to guard my expression.

"What is it?" Bub asked, propping the gardening tools against the wheelbarrow so he could take me by the shoulders. "Are you all right? We don't have to go if the idea upsets you."

"I think we do." I winced. "Something… happened at work today, after I dropped my scythe off at Warren's."

Before Bub could ask, the hounds bellowed out a warning, Saul's deeper howl beginning a split-second before Coreen's. The effect had a doorbell quality—but we never got unexpected company this far off the grid.

Bub snatched up a pair of trowels from his gardening supplies. My hand went to the borrowed scythe at my hip, though I stopped short of hitting the release button. Even Warren's forgiveness had its limits.

"Ding-dong! Demon calling," a sweet, familiar voice sing-songed. Then Amy rounded the side of the house in a slinky pencil skirt and sleeveless turtleneck.

Gabriel's on-again, off-again girlfriend looked as if she'd come straight from a Hell Committee meeting, which I would have bet my last coin was the case. A bottle of dark wine lay in the crook of one arm, and she waved her other in the air as she spoke.

"Sorry to bother you so late in the evening." Her barbed tail curled around one of her legs as she took in our defensive postures. "Cindy Morningstar insisted that I drop by tonight. She would have come herself, but she—"

"Can't stomach crow?" I finished.

Amy gave us a pained smile and held out the bottle of wine. "Here. This is from Lucifer's private cellar."

"What's the occasion?" Bub asked, finally discarding the trowels in his wheelbarrow to accept the wine. He shot a curious glance in my direction, clearly having decided this visit was no more a coincidence than Persephone's dinner invitation. Amy's gaze darted between us.

"Oh, you haven't told him yet," she surmised. "This is a bit awkward."

"Would someone spit it out already?" Bub huffed and handed the bottle to me. I echoed his annoyance with a huff of my own.

"I *just* got home." I made a face at him and turned back to Amy. "Word certainly travels fast in the underworld. It's barely been an hour since Jenni broke the news to me."

"What news?" Bub snapped.

"The council wants me to fetch original believers for them again."

Amy barked out a nervous laugh. "Don't sell yourself so short." She held her hands up at Bub's narrowed glare. "It's not like that."

"Then what *is* it like?" he demanded. "And how is she supposed to accomplish that when the council revoked her throne-given abilities?"

"Turns out"—Amy gave me an apologetic smile— "that's not entirely true. Is it?"

Well, crap.

Bub's wounded expression made my insides clench with guilt. It wasn't that I hadn't trusted him enough to tell him about the gifts Naledi had opted to leave me with. I just hadn't needed to use them in ten years, so it didn't seem worth sharing.

"I can't see original believers," I explained, "but they can *allegedly* still see me perimortem."

Amy nodded encouragingly. "Which means you're in the unique position to help us find one to serve as a resident guest of dishonor in Hell. It's the only way we can fortify our borders and prevent hellcats and rogue demons from randomly crossing over to the mortal side—or infesting the adjoining afterlives, like this one."

"And Cindy sent you over here to bury the hatchet so I would be more inclined to help?" I hitched an eyebrow at Amy, daring her to deny it. Her smile stretched wider, but her eyes betrayed her eager anxiety.

"There was some concern that you might be unwilling. But this is a mutually beneficial scenario, wouldn't you agree?" she said, clasping her hands together as if in prayer. "And the Hell Committee is prepared to offer you a handsome bonus in addition to the council's bid."

"How handsome?" Bub asked, sparing me the effort. It was more curiosity than greed. Knowing would make it clear how much faith the council had in me. Maalik's offer on Khadija's behalf was one thing… but Cindy Morningstar? That was quite another.

Amy opened her hands. "Name your price."

In the stunned silence that followed, the lanterns hanging around the garden and patio flickered to life, cutting through the settling darkness. Frogs croaked from the water garden surrounding Ursula's pond, and crickets that had escaped the predatory plants chirped a song of victory.

"Bloody hell." Bub pinched the bridge of his nose. "How many afterlives are relying on Lana to fetch them a resident believer?"

"Three, for now," Amy answered. "All in the underworld region—Hell, Tartarus, and Jahannam."

I felt Bub's gaze migrate toward me again, but to his credit, he bit his forked tongue. I knew the question that would come later.

We all started as the manor's back door opened, and Rupert stepped out onto the patio. The pair of stacked horns at the apex of his forehead made him look like a proud rhinoceros. His eyes widened at the sight of Amy, and his cheeks flushed as he addressed the Lord of the Flies. "Shall I set another place at the table, Master Beelzebub?"

"It's tempting," Bub said under his breath, earning an elbow to the ribs from me.

"Thank you, but I can't stay," Amy answered, giving Rupert a curious frown.

"Very well." Rupert bowed again. "Dinner is served," he added before retreating inside the house.

Amy cleared her throat and turned back to us, clasping her hands together again. "So… this has been productive, yeah?"

I rolled my eyes. "Sure."

"Perfect!" Amy beamed, ignoring my sarcasm. "I'll tell Cindy she can expect an official quote from you before the assignment begins." She blew an air kiss and wiggled her fingers as she backed away. "Ta-ta!"

Once she'd disappeared around the side of the house, Bub staked me with another accusing stare.

"Well, this explains Persephone's dinner invitation," he said, propping his hands on his hips. "I guess that just leaves a representative from Jahannam. I wonder who they'll send."

"Maalik. And they're offering three times the council's bid if I give their soul priority—and if I don't sell it on the new-and-improved ghost market," I answered bluntly. "It's been a very, *very* long day."

"I'll say." Bub rubbed a hand over his face and scratched his bearded jaw. Then he grabbed the bottle of wine from me. "At least we've got something strong to wash down this supposed *dinner* we're about to have."

"It wasn't that bad!" I insisted as I followed him up the patio steps and inside the house.

Things were about to get complicated, and I definitely wouldn't have the patience to adjust to yet another new butler anytime soon. Though I secretly hoped Rupert had made plenty of garlic bread.

CHAPTER SIX

"As you ramble on through life, whatever be your goal,
keep your eye on the donut, and not on the hole."
—*The Optimist's Creed of Mayflower Donuts*

THE COFFEE FROM NESSA'S donut shop tasted like Christmas with bits of peppermint and cinnamon sprinkled over the mound of whipped cream she'd piled on top. I breathed in the piping-hot, sugary goodness and resisted the urge to skip down the docks with a box of equally sugary donuts balanced in my opposite hand.

I was earlier than usual, but I wanted to get a jumpstart on the day since I'd be leaving most of the workload to my apprentices. Jenni had Regina shuffle some harvests around so Kevin and Eliza wouldn't have anything too challenging to tackle without me. I'd already picked out the more questionable medium-risk jobs and planned to take care of them myself before breaking off to meet with Jenni.

What I hadn't planned on was catching my apprentices buck-naked and tangled in a bedsheet atop the hatch platform of my ship. Kevin's mop of dark curls lay over Eliza's shoulder, his face buried in the crook of her neck, yielding a throaty moan that had drowned out my gasp of surprise. It was the box of donuts dropping to the deck floor that finally caught their attention.

"Oh!" Eliza squealed, dragging the sheet with her as she rolled off the platform. Kevin grasped for a corner of the sheet but was too late. I turned away long enough to give him time to cover himself with a pillow.

"It's like forty degrees out here. What the hell is wrong with you two?"

"We had a blanket," Kevin said, searching the deck floor beneath the platform. Tom and Felix, the pair of helljacks Kevin had kept from Coreen's litter, yipped at us from the poop deck. Kevin scowled up at them. "A little late now."

"How long has this been going on?" I asked, feeling completely out of touch. Why was I always the last to know these things?

"Uh…" Kevin made a strangled noise in the back of his throat. "You mean the sex?"

"Since last night," Eliza snapped, covering her face with her free hand to hide her embarrassment. She raked her fingers through her short afro before adding in a gentler voice, "I'm so sorry, boss. It won't happen again."

"Really? It won't?" Kevin pouted.

I bent down to retrieve the box of donuts, cracking the lid to inspect them. Thankfully, they'd survived the ride. "I don't care what or who you do in your free time," I said. "Just maybe don't do it right out in the open. Come on, guys. Anyone could have walked up that ramp and gotten a peep show."

"Got it." Eliza pointed a finger at me. "I'll just grab a quick shower and put on some clothes," she added as Kevin scooted off the platform.

"Ditto," he said, then nodded at the donut box. "Save me a chocolate one."

I averted my gaze again as he trotted off toward the main cabin, a pillow held over his crotch. Eliza chewed her bottom lip as she stared after him. Her dark skin glistened with sweat despite the frigid temperature, but I doubted the shiver that shook her shoulders had anything to do with the cold.

"Boston cream still your favorite?" I asked, breaking her lusty daze.

"What?" She blinked at me and then the donuts. "Oh! Yeah. That's perfect. I'll… be right back."

I half expected her to follow Kevin, but she made a beeline for the forecastle cabin. Maybe they really were a new thing. Good for them.

If Eliza dated, it wasn't something she'd ever shared with me. She'd graduated from the Reaper Academy with top marks, which meant she likely hadn't found time to get mixed up in the Limbo City dating scene.

Kevin hadn't dated anyone since Josie's death. It was time for him to get back on the horse, so to speak. Of course, workplace relationships had their share of complications. That he and Eliza were both training under the same mentor could prove disastrous if whatever this was didn't last. And as that shared mentor, I was sure I'd end up shipwrecked in the aftermath, too. But I didn't have time to worry about that today.

Soon, my apprentices returned with damp hair and fresh robes. Kevin had found time to fix a pot of coffee and handed a cup to Eliza before having at the donut box I'd set on the corner of the hatch platform—on the opposite side from where I'd found them. A spot they hopefully hadn't stickied while consummating their budding romance.

As they ate, I explained why I'd crashed their naked boat party and what the day would look like after I left them to go off on the council's new quest. Kevin, who'd been present along with Ellen the last time I'd encountered a pre-mortem original believer, was none too surprised. I had the feeling he'd expected this and had been waiting for it. Which was a relief because navigating Eliza's reaction required my full attention.

"That sounds super high-risk. Shouldn't you have backup? Why aren't we coming with you?" she rapid-fired, the skin between her brows puckering more with each question. The fact that she was so eager to help, dangers be damned, plucked at my heartstrings. Maybe I wasn't doing half-bad as a mentor. I grinned and squeezed her shoulder.

"I'm sure I'll have backup—of some sort." Bub's winged spies were stealthier these days, but after the events of the previous evening, I had no doubt a fly had hitched a ride over from Tartarus. But I wouldn't out my guardian demon just yet. "Jenni can't afford to pull three reapers off the job right now, at least not on such short notice. I'll be careful," I added as Eliza's hand pressed over mine, pinning it to her arm in a tender gesture.

"We'll work fast today," she insisted. "If we get through the harvests early, you know you can count on us to help."

Kevin nodded in agreement and waved his digital docket at me. "These morgue and funeral home pickups will be a breeze. The rest shouldn't be too bad, but I'll put the helljacks to work and speed things along."

"You two are the best." I toasted them with my coffee before polishing it off and then glanced at my watch. We were well ahead of schedule. I just hoped we could keep it that way.

Kevin's note about bringing the helljacks made me long for my hounds. But they were at Hades' Hound

House this morning, getting the stink scrubbed off. They'd be back to work soon enough.

I left my apprentices to finish their coffee and headed down to the dock, where I coined off to my first job of the day.

Harvesting souls in the Free World made my job a real grab bag. Don't get me wrong—democracy and tolerance were great and all, but back when kings imposed their religious views on the general populace, it wasn't unusual to end up with a docket full of souls bound for one of three simple destinations: a single paradise, a single underworld, or the Sea of Eternity.

Nowadays, I could collect a Buddhist from a cancer wing, hop a city over and grab a Wiccan from a house fire, then walk three blocks to pick up a Christian at a graveside service. I didn't mind the variety of harvests, but the delivery to a dozen different afterlives pushed my workdays into overtime.

As much as I'd resisted having an apprentice, I had to admit that letting Kevin and Eliza take over delivery duties now and then was a welcome perk. Today, it was a necessary one.

I spent the better half of my morning in Toronto and New York, collecting souls fresh from their deathbeds— or crime scenes. Medium-risk generally meant a fifty-fifty chance they'd evacuate their bodies without reaper intervention. The timing was more precise than the laid-back, low-risk harvests I preferred, but the pay was better.

My last stop was an interstate crash site in the Midwest, where a whitetail buck had jumped in front of a church bus. There might have been more survivors if the driver hadn't swerved into oncoming traffic. It made for an easy pickup, anyway. And at least one soul's Off-Broadway dreams were about to come true since they were determined to perform their traveling Christmas pageant for a heavenly audience.

I shepherded the cluster of Heaven-bound souls back to Limbo City and down into the hold of the ship, setting them up with board games and Bibles before locking up the hatch. It would be a few hours until the rest of the day's catch joined them, and my apprentices set sail for the afterlives.

I went ahead and traded my work robe for my leather jacket and headed into the city. Looking the part of Death just didn't seem like the best idea while encountering souls that could potentially see me. I didn't feel like running down my marks today.

With the lunch rush an hour off, the harbor was quiet. A few dryads unloaded a merchant ship, and a nephilim guard used his spear to shoo away a stork as it poked its head inside the travel booth near the dock entrance. Market Street was livelier. The vendors busied themselves tidying and restocking their tables in preparation for the next wave of patrons.

My handful of harvests had kept me on my toes, and I was already running late. So, I stood in line at the travel booth, taking my turn after a cherub with a broken harp tucked under one arm and a briefcase in his other hand. I hated to waste the coin, but shaving five blocks off my trip meant avoiding a lecture from Jenni for being tardy.

The booth spat me out on a corner between the Reaper Academy and Reapers Inc. I crossed the street and entered the building, trying to ignore the sweat coating my palms.

Jenni's message had been vague, simply requesting that I report to her office after the council meeting. She hadn't mentioned who else would be present, but I had a feeling I wouldn't be going out to collect such precious cargo without some sort of supervision.

Of all the people I dreaded running into, I hadn't expected to find Ellen waiting for me in the lobby. Dark bags hung under her eyes, and her curls were a frizzy mess—which was extra alarming considering her usual high level of maintenance.

"I really thought she already knew," Ellen blurted as soon as she noticed me. My teeth clenched involuntarily, but I refrained from making a scene and headed for the elevators.

Ellen followed, wringing her hands as she blubbered. "I… I wanted to apologize in person."

I ignored her and punched the button to call an elevator. This wasn't the time or place.

"It's just that Ross is under so much pressure, and the Guard is really struggling to keep up with all the hellcat reports. He thinks the only way to secure the borders is to restore the throne—"

"I'm not restoring the throne," I finally interjected. An elevator pinged, the triangular light above its doors lighting as it began to open.

"Why not?" Ellen snapped, dropping her repentant façade. "Because a handful of nonbelievers think you're something special?"

"Do they now?" I spared her a sideways glance as I waited for the elevator to empty. The lobby was by no means full, but it was crowded enough that Ellen's tone had garnered a few curious stares. The attention seemed to embolden her.

"What have those souls ever actually done for you? Stop being so damn selfish, Lana."

"Wow." I shook my head and stepped inside the elevator, turning to face her as I pressed the button for the seventy-fifth floor. "Thanks for the in-person apology. I'm touched. Really." I placed a hand over my heart as the doors closed, leaving Ellen to sort out her guilt and fury on her own.

CHAPTER SEVEN

*"How well I have learned that there is no fence to sit on
between Heaven and Hell. There is a deep, wide gulf, a chasm,
and in that chasm is no place for any man."*
—*Johnny Cash*

As uncalled for as Ellen's ambush in the lobby
had been, it didn't stop my conscience from attempting
to eat me alive on the ride up in the elevator.

Selfish? Was that really what she thought of me? After
everything I'd done to safeguard Limbo City? After all
I'd lost in the process of bringing about Khadija's vision
for the future of Eternity?

And how the hell was I supposed to know that the
remnants of the skill the council had nearly crucified me
for having in the first place was the fix for this latest
trouble in paradise?

I still wasn't entirely convinced that was the case. But
I was here, wasn't I? No one had dragged me inside the
building, kicking and screaming.

By the time the elevator opened on the top floor, my face hurt from scowling. Regina glanced up from the front desk, her brows knitting and wings contracting at my sour demeanor.

"President Fang said you could go on in." She nodded at Jenni's closed office door. I dipped my chin in thanks, too afraid my bad mood would spill into my tone and that my words would cut her. She was fragile for a nephilim, and I'd already made her cry once. I wasn't about to make a habit of it.

I rapped my knuckles on the door before entering Jenni's office, and my mood instantly lifted. Only one angel had that effect on me.

"Hey, pilgrim." Gabriel's face broke into a cheesy grin as he wrapped an arm around my back, squeezing me in a half-hug. "Heard you could use some backup."

Well, that explained the clean linen pants and matching shirt.

Gabriel's return to the political arena had been short-lived, though he was in better standing with Peter these days and took more frequent trips to the mortal side. Of course, he had a white robe for those jobs. He preferred grungy drawstring pants and going shirtless so his massive wings weren't restricted during his time off. This new outfit was a compromise between the two.

"How'd you get roped into this gig?" I smiled at him, momentarily forgetting my frustration at being dubbed the council's lapdog. Gabriel made everything better. How I'd landed him as my backup without begging and pleading was an anomaly bordering on a miracle.

"Mary asked me personally—at Holly's request, I'm sure." He smirked and tossed his head back, brushing a golden curl out of his face.

"Only after pressure from Cindy and Maalik," Jenni added from behind her desk. "They're both eager to secure the borders of their afterlives and get this hellcat outbreak under control. The entire council is in agreement that you're our best option, Lana."

"And I'm the honey they're hoping to catch you with," Gabriel said with a wink. The mention of honey made me wonder if Bub's tagalong fly had waited outside. Sending a covert spy into Reapers Inc. was risky— especially if he didn't want to be accused of treason again.

"I suppose that makes me the vinegar," a deep, silky voice concluded, drawing my attention to a dark corner of the room.

I hadn't seen Hecate in quite some time, but she wasn't the kind of goddess easily forgotten. Long, black hair spilled over her shoulders, almost vanishing against her velvet blouse. Her dress slacks and loafers were more business-casual, though she looked like a gothic cover model with her high-arching brows and full mouth. Silver key charms dangled from a long chain around her neck, jingling as she stood and crossed the room to join us.

"Hades and Persephone thought I might be of use given my liminal nature and chthonic abilities," Hecate said, extending her hand in greeting. Her grip was icy, but it was her dark eyes that sent a shiver through me.

"I appreciate the help," I said diplomatically, earning a nod of approval from Jenni.

"Hecate has already secured the Fates' blessing," Jenni said, turning her attention to a digital docket on her desk. She clicked a few buttons, and my docket buzzed in response, vibrating in my back pocket.

"Blessing for what, exactly?" I asked, retrieving the device to review the destinations list.

"To expedite the death of the original believers you identify," Hecate answered.

I blinked at her, speechless. The time of deities inflicting death upon mortals was ancient history—except for Atropos, who was responsible for programming the deaths of recycled souls at the factory she co-managed with her sisters. Which I suppose explained why Hecate had needed their blessing.

"I know how cruel this must seem," Jenni said, voicing what I couldn't in my shock, "especially considering how we'll then peel their lives back to their least-admirable incarnations and send them to their respective underworlds. But casualties of the Second War of

Eternity included so many original believers, and the ones we seek now are quite specific. We can't possibly afford to wait until one perishes in their own time."

"They will be justly rewarded for their sacrifice and service," Hecate said, her dark eyes watching me with guarded curiosity.

I wasn't sure what to make of her yet. As a goddess of the crossroads and ghosts, she was undoubtedly an ideal fit for the assignment. But considering her rising popularity among the modern witches, this all seemed beneath her. I understood Gabriel's involvement. We had history, and I'd been there for him through his periodic falls from grace.

What reason did Zeus's most honored goddess have for dirtying her hands with reaper-level grunt work? I had a hard time buying that it was simply a favor to Hades and Persephone, but I wasn't about to voice my skepticism with those scary-ass eyes drinking me in.

"Okay then." I cleared my throat and looked down at the list on my docket. "Looks like we have three stops in New Orleans, so we can start there."

"Sounds good to me," Gabriel chirped. "Work smarter, not harder."

"Agreed," Hecate said, folding her hands behind her back. A soft smile tugged at her lips, and a puzzle piece shifted in my brain.

"Just out of curiosity, which original believers are we searching for?" I asked, turning my attention back to Jenni. She sat up straighter in her chair, her neutral expression suddenly growing edges.

"I don't see how that information will help," she said. "I know the research is a bit lacking, but most evidence still suggests that previous lives have no bearing on current incarnations."

"Humor me." I smiled, daring her to refuse the simple request given what she and the council were asking me to do. She held my stare a second longer before caving.

"Sure. Why not?" She laced her fingers together on her desk and sucked in a deep breath. "Hell has requested Judas Iscariot. Cindy will be sponsoring his stay at a presidential suite at the Inferno Chateau with a team of… bodyguards."

Bodyguards? I supposed that sounded nicer than *jailers*.

"Judas was reinserted about a thousand years back," Gabriel explained. "I'm sure he'll just be glad he's not returning to the ninth circle."

"Let's hope so," Jenni said.

Her uncertainty made me wonder if the souls would have some say in the matter. Would an original believer do any good if they weren't cooperative? If willingness didn't matter, would they be locked up for however long the council deemed their presence necessary? Would I be expected to replace them from time to time like the throne soul, or would they last longer with only the weight of a single afterlife resting on their shoulders?

I had so many questions, but we were trying to solve a unique problem. I imagined the council was waiting for answers, too—answers that *no one* would have until I delivered these rare souls. The strain in Jenni's face suggested she was tired of fielding such questions, so I kept them to myself as she continued.

"Then there's Zaynab, the woman who served Muhammad the poisoned lamb."

"But wasn't she Jewish?" My schooling from the academy was a hazy memory, but Foundational Faiths had been one of the very first classes I'd taken before I became jaded and disillusioned.

"She was." Jenni nodded. "But she saw her failure as proof that Muhammad was a true prophet, and so she believed in and feared the Islamic hell. Regardless, we've secured permissions from both Shamayim and Sheol. Everyone wants to see this problem resolved."

"Fair enough." I shrugged. "Who do we have for Tartarus?"

Jenni's pregnant pause made my breath tighten in my chest. This was the detail she didn't want to share. The thing she suspected I wouldn't be pleased to discover.

"Tantalus." Jenni's nose twitched as if she were resisting the urge to scrunch it in disgust. I did it for her and added a shudder for good measure.

"Ew." The ancient king who had killed and cooked one of his own sons, serving him to the Olympian gods for dinner, was one of the notorious three who had suffered long sentences in Tartarus for their crimes. I wasn't looking forward to having him back in my neck of the underworld.

"It will be an adjustment, to be sure," Hecate said, cocking her head thoughtfully. "But he'll finally get to taste the fruit of the tree he was cursed to stand under for all those centuries."

"And who will be sponsoring the cannibal chef?" I asked, fairly sure I didn't want to know the answer.

Jenni's lips pressed together in a grim line. "That's ultimately up to Hades and Persephone... but I hear they're having their guesthouse renovated."

"Super." I looked back down at the docket, taking in the list of scheduled stops with new eyes. The original believers hadn't been noted for each potential candidate, probably to deter favoritism—in the event I was offered a bribe. But though Jenni had been right about the convoluted evidence, patterns could still be found.

New Orleans had a heavy pagan population, lots of witches who celebrated and worshipped deities like

Hecate. If their past lives had any influence at all, those souls were most likely potential candidates for Tantalus.

If today's harvest yielded the OG Hannibal Lecter, the dinner party with the neighbors was a definite no-go.

CHAPTER EIGHT

*"There is an eternal landscape, a geography of the soul;
we search for its outlines all our lives."*
—*Josephine Hart*

THE IDEA OF HARVESTING a soul before its time was a nagging thorn in my conscience that persisted even as Gabriel, Hecate, and I strolled the French Quarter in search of our first mark. This wasn't right, no matter where the chosen souls were destined to go or when they were meant to go there.

People changed. They repented and atoned or were lured to the dark side. But until they did, they hadn't earned what destiny held in store for them—especially not some halfway fate of living the high life in the underworld. Whatever direction they were headed, I couldn't shake how perverse this assignment felt. It insulted the integrity of my psychopomp existence.

At least I had found consolation in the fact that we would only be harvesting three souls. Those who couldn't see me pre-mortem were off the hook, free to live their lives until destiny caught up with them. They'd never know of this early brush with Death.

The sun was high above us, shining brightly between the buildings. Most of the shops and bars hadn't opened yet, and the sidewalks were empty. Despite the mild temperatures and holiday decorations, December was quiet in New Orleans. Tourism wouldn't pick up again until Mardi Gras season began.

"There," Hecate said, pointing out a sign that hung from the second-floor balcony of a café where several patrons enjoyed an early lunch. "That's where Tonya Reeves works."

"Uh… yeah." I resisted asking how she'd come by the information. When we arrived a street over, all I'd offered was the soul's name and that she worked nearby. I hadn't seen Jenni give Hecate a digital docket or file, but perhaps the Fates had briefed her.

Gabriel scratched the back of his head. "I guess you're not waiting for a death cue this time. How do you want to do this?"

Another pang of wrongness struck me as I stared at the café. Three hundred years of waiting for nature to take its course was not an easy instinct to shrug off.

"I guess I'll just wander around in there until I bump into her?" I said, wondering if my lack of confidence could be any more obvious. I made for the café's entrance, stopping short when I realized that Hecate was following me.

"I was instructed to stay close by," she said, politely ignoring my skeptical frown.

"Right. Sure." A whisper of a laugh wheezed past my lips. Like I was dumb enough to tell a goddess of her stature what she could and couldn't do.

Gabriel scratched his head again as if he were considering whether he should join us. My discomfort with Hecate's proximity seemed to make up his mind. He stretched his wings wide and lifted into the air.

"I'll keep watch from outside," he said, ascending toward the balcony. The wind he created ruffled tablecloths and sent guests snatching for runaway napkins, though they ignored the angel perched on the balcony railing.

Gabriel could appear and disappear at will amongst the mortals, but the peace treaty signed after the First War of Eternity mandated that all divine beings were to obtain a permit first. Even then, they restricted their exposure to believers of their own faith.

The older deities like Hecate had strict limitations, as well. If humans wanted a glimpse of their patron god or goddess, ancient traditions had to be upheld and ceremonies performed. Long gone were the days of Olympians playing footsie with the mortals and practically living in their backyard.

I stuffed my hands into the pockets of my jacket and turned back to the front of the café. Hecate opened her arm, inviting me to enter ahead of her. I accepted the invitation with a nod and slipped through the French doors. The cool glass tickled my skin as it yielded to my soul matter without so much as disturbing the bell anchored above.

Hecate entered a step behind me. As a goddess, she was undoubtedly well-versed in phantom mechanics. However, I imagined the knowledge was ingrained in her mythic DNA rather than instilled via a boring academy course as mine had been. She probably didn't have any trouble passing through solid walls either.

Cajun spices tickled my nose, and jazz music bubbled over the hum of small talk from more patrons dining inside the café. I spotted the single waitress tending to this level, quickly noting the name badge that read *Samantha*. I leaned over the table she bussed to get a better look at her face, just to be sure. Some souls went by their middle names or a nickname.

"That's not her," Hecate said matter-of-factly. "She's upstairs."

"Oh?" I bit back a snippy retort. With two apprentices, I was used to being the most informed person on any given job.

I followed the goddess through the dining room, weaving between the tightly packed tables and chairs. We passed a display wall with vintage fishing gear, nets, and crawfish traps, before reaching a dark stairwell tucked into the corner. Once again, Hecate motioned for me to take the lead.

"I guess your file on the soul included more details than the one I received," I said, doing my best to inflect a neutral tone as we climbed the stairs.

"No one gave me a file," Hecate admitted. "Tonya's coven is blood sworn to me."

I paused on a narrow landing and turned to face her. The dim bulb hanging above us in the stairwell painted dark shadows across her eyes, leaving only a freckle of light in each, like the first and brightest stars of nightfall. Standing this close, I had to crane my neck to look up at her.

"You'd kill one of your followers?" I whispered the question as if someone might overhear. Sacrificing a personal adherent felt profane on any level, but for a deity like Hecate, who had fewer to spare than the modern gods...

"It was a condition of the Fates," she said, her voice nearly as quiet as mine. "The other committees are eager to resolve this. But make no mistake, they would not forfeit a soul of such value without exacting a heavy price from the Summerland Society. This is the only way. Besides, anyone of my cult will understand and come willingly."

I appreciated her honesty. I still didn't like the idea of King Creepy living next door, but maybe the soul would retain whatever decency it had learned in this lifetime, as Winston had before having his lives wound back to his King Tut incarnation. Or maybe having Hecate nearby would at least curb his homicidal kitchen antics.

I turned to continue up the stairs and came face-to-face with a full tray of dirty dishes. My breath caught as I attempted to slip between the veils and out of the way, but I was too slow. The tray scuffed my shoulder and angled upward. Everything slid one way and then the other before crashing to the floor. Broken plates and cups spilled down the stairs below us, and bits of food and cold coffee splattered the walls.

"*Sonofabitch.*" The unfortunate waitress who had been carrying the tray was our mark. There was just enough light in the crowded stairwell that I could read her name tag. Tonya grasped her head with both hands and swore again. "I am so fucking fired," she hissed.

"Say something to her," Hecate suggested. "We have to be sure she's not simply ignoring you because she's in shock."

"Right." I blinked at the girl, my mind going rigid with doubt as I tried to figure out the best way to engage. "Helloooo?"

"You'd better keep your mouth shut," Tonya snapped, sending me back a step.

"Excuse y—"

"Seriously?" Another voice cut me off as it echoed up through the stairwell. "I bet the entire damn Quarter heard that racket." Samantha, the waitress from the main-level dining room, stood at the foot of the stairs with her hands on her hips.

I glanced over my shoulder at Hecate and groaned when she nudged me toward Tonya. This was getting awkward. It couldn't possibly be so difficult to get a waitress's attention. Could it?

"Hey!" I tried again, jumping up and down on the landing. "I'm gonna tell your boss that you spit in my food!" I wiggled my fingers in Tonya's face and wailed like a banshee.

"Okay," Hecate interjected, wincing at my shrill tone. "I think we're done here. For now. I'm sure I'll have to return later when she calls on me to help her find a new job," she added as Tonya stormed down the stairs, snarling more profanities at her colleague.

"Sorry about that." I gave Hecate a tight smile that was only half genuine and tiptoed through the obstacle course of broken dishes on the stairs, moving past the bickering waitresses.

One soul down, seventeen to go.

CHAPTER NINE

"When men destroy their old gods
they will find new ones to take their place."
—Pearl S. Buck

WHAT A COMPLETE AND utter waste of a day.

I supposed I'd asked for this with my hesitation to harvest a soul whose life had ended prematurely. But there was no satisfaction to be had when it meant I'd be sent out to try again tomorrow. Jenni's disbelieving ire didn't help matters either.

I slouched in one of her guest chairs and folded my arms over my stomach as she paced back and forth in her office. Gabriel stood in front of the wall of windows, squinting into the distance as if he could glimpse the future in the horizon over the sea. He moved to rest his arm on the glass above his head, but Jenni swatted him away.

"I just had the windows cleaned," she snapped, ruining his pensive brooding. Gabriel fluttered back a step and rolled his eyes.

"Can we leave now?" he whined. "I'm starving."

"You're always starving." Jenni turned away from him and crossed the room again, stopping at her desk to stare down at me. "You're absolutely certain none of them could see you?" she asked for the zillionth time.

"We're positive," Hecate answered before I had a chance to tell Jenni what I'd do to her damn windows if she didn't lay off with the third degree. The goddess of the crossroads stood in the corner opposite Gabriel, away from the windows where the evening light didn't touch. "We tested each soul at least twice," she explained—and not for the first time.

"I just don't get it." Jenni dropped into her chair and propped her elbows on her desk. She yanked the chopstick out of her tightly wound bun and raked her fingers through her hair with a disheartened sigh. "Those were the Fates' top candidates. We'll have to request a new selection. The council meeting is going to be a nightmare in the morning." She groaned and pressed her fingers over her closed eyelids as if she were fighting off a migraine.

"You know what *I* don't get?" I said, my annoyance coming to a head. "How none of this seemed like that big of a deal until you found out that original believers *might* be able to see me. If it turns out that my gift has faded away along with the throne realm, what's the council's backup plan? What were they prepared to do before I was thrown into the mix?"

Gabriel's face flushed as he turned toward the window again, giving me his back. Not a great sign. Jenni finally pulled her hands away from her eyes to look at me. "I don't know that I'd call it a plan, exactly."

"But it is," Hecate said, her smooth voice unwavering. "It's the oldest plan in nearly every sacred text."

A creeping sensation prickled its way up my spine until it reached my neck, cuing a shiver. "No way. Things can't possibly be that bad. Can they?" I directed the question at Gabriel's reflection in the window, where I could see him watching me from the corner of his eye.

"Not yet," he said softly, his breath fogging the glass.

Jenni scowled at him and went back to massaging her eyelids. "But we're not far off," she countered. "If we can't stop the flow of demons into the mortal realm, the gods will have no choice but to unleash the armies of heaven. It's all downhill from there—and despite the puppies and rainbows the scriptures detail in the aftermath, there's no guarantee that Eternity has enough soul matter to sustain such an idealistic utopia."

"Meaning…?" I blinked at her, but it was Hecate who answered.

"Meaning we could have our very own end times to deal with on this side of the grave."

"And no one to save us," Gabriel finished.

I'd thought Jenni's speech about helping all of Eternity was a bunch of bologna. Just another sad attempt by the council to reclaim the power and prestige they'd lost. The hefty bribes and lack of red tape made more sense now.

"At least we have the Nephilim Guard to keep the demons at bay for now," I said, clinging to what little shred of optimism I could muster.

"The Guard is running on fumes and filling Meng Po's infirmary." Leave it to Jenni to ruin a perfectly good delusion. "Ross is ready to resign," she continued. "He lost thirty guards yesterday alone. Experienced, senior nephilim. Like Abe."

"Abe?" I sucked in a sharp breath and pressed a hand over my heart.

The guard was mainly assigned dock duty, but he'd been a part of my security detail after rebels torched my old apartment. He'd also joined my team when the council ordered me to dismantle the ghost market. We hadn't worked closely since, but he dropped by the ship for poker night whenever he wasn't working. I knew his favorite pizza was anchovy and that his left wing was bigger than his right—something he was self-conscious about. Now, he was just… gone?

Jenni sighed and fixed her bloodshot eyes on the window, staring out at whatever troubling nothing had captured Gabriel's attention. "We also lost two reapers today. Molly Driver and her apprentice. I know you only worked together on the Posy Unit for a short while, but you seemed fond of her."

"I was." I rubbed at the growing ache in my chest and took a deep breath.

This couldn't be happening. Yesterday, I'd harvested killer clowns and drunks who went skinny dipping with piranhas. Now, my friends were dropping like flies, and the world was falling apart—and everyone expected *me* to fix it.

"If this assignment is so important, and the demons are becoming such a problem, we should have a larger team," I said.

Jenni's brow furrowed. "I'm sorry, but we can't afford to pull your apprentices off task. It's been a busy year, and everyone is already overworked."

"What about Tasha Henry?"

"What about her?" Jenni snapped.

"You said it yourself. Everyone is overworked. And she deserves to be pardoned anyway after what she did to help take down the ghost market."

Jenni scoffed. "The only reason she knew so much about the ghost market was because she'd dealt with them to sell poached souls. The council will never agree to excuse her previous crimes. Besides, the Guard hasn't reported a sighting in five years. No one knows where she is."

"If they locate her, do you think the council would reconsider?" I asked.

If ever there were a time to secure a ticket home for Tasha, it was now. She didn't complain as vocally as Ellen about being stuck out of her element, but I knew it bothered her, living on the mortal side among people she couldn't interact with—at least no more than a hostile ghost could. It had to be so incredibly lonely. Not that she'd ever admit it to me.

"The Guard has enough on their plate right now," Jenni said, exhaustion finally dropping her shoulders away from her ears. "Go home. Get some sleep, if you can. We'll meet up tomorrow morning after the council arrives. I should have a new list from the Fates by then."

She reached for her desk phone as I stood. Gabriel finally turned away from the window. He placed a hand on my shoulder and followed me out of Jenni's office. Hecate nodded to us, but she remained behind. As the liaison for the Fates, I expected that Jenni wasn't quite done with her yet.

Until the borders of hell were secure, and the apocalypse was put back on the shelf, I knew I wouldn't feel *done* about anything.

The lobby was dark, lit only by the fading daylight through the wall of windows on the opposite side of the building from Jenni's office. Regina had left for the day.

"Come on," Gabriel said, steering me past the front desk and toward the elevators. "I'll buy the first round at Purgatory."

"Sure," I agreed before remembering my dinner plans with Bub. "I can only stay for one, but I'll get you back next poker night." *If we live that long,* I thought.

Gabriel seemed plenty depressed without me adding to the doom and gloom, but I could tell there was something more bothering him that he hadn't shared in front of the others. Hopefully, a single beer would be enough to drag it out of him.

It was Thursday, so the early crowd at Purgatory Lounge was light. A few off-duty guards dined in the row of booths that sectioned off the empty dance floor, and a handful of factory souls lingered between the jukebox and pool tables, dropping quarters and fries as they cheered for some mortal football team playing on the big screen.

Gabriel and I sat at the bar like we always did when it was just the two of us. Xaphen was usually good company, but he was short a waitress tonight. He popped in and out of the kitchen, his hands full of appetizers and pitchers of Ambrosia Ale. The crown of flames that circled his head flickered excitedly as he darted throughout the room, trying to keep everyone happy until the late staff arrived.

I let Gabriel make it to the bottom of his mug before interrupting whatever deep thoughts were holding his attention hostage. He hadn't said two words since we arrived, which was rare even when Amy's father was tending the bar.

"You really think this could be it, don't you?" I swirled the last inch of beer in my glass, deciding that I didn't have the stomach for it. There wasn't enough alcohol in Eternity to make the end of the world palatable.

"I wish I could say I didn't believe that." Gabriel sighed and trailed a finger through the condensation on his mug, refusing to look at me. "But there are other signs to consider."

"Such as?"

"The plagues and fires." He rolled his hand in the air. "I know it's all open to interpretation, and the mortals can never seem to agree on the when and where, but... some of the demon sightings have reported beasts that look like lions."

"You mean hellcats?" I hooked an elbow over the back of my seat and tried to keep a straight face when he glared at me.

"More so than the typical hellcat," he said. "'The heads of the horses resembled the heads of lions, and out of their mouths came fire, smoke, and sulfur.'"

I couldn't contain my groan this time. "It must be dire if you're quoting Revelations at me."

"This is serious." Gabriel's brow creased. "And it's worth noting that these troops with lion-headed mounts appear right after a fallen star is given a key to the abyss to release the scorpion-tailed locusts of Abaddon."

"Have there been reports of those, too?" I asked.

Gabriel's jaw flexed. He dragged his gaze away from mine and reached for the pitcher to refill his mug. "Not yet, but I fear it's only a matter of time."

"Doubtful," Xaphen grumbled, having caught the tail end of our conversation. He circled the counter and took the empty pitcher from Gabriel. "When I left the abyss, Abaddon was training his pests to farm netherye and brimcorn for Lucifer's latest whiskey venture."

"Oh, that's just great." The information only seemed to agitate the angel. "Let's turn the master of the locusts into a lush. I can't see anything going wrong with that plan."

Xaphen snorted. "Says the angel slamming beers in a demon-run bar." His eyebrows bobbed up on his forehead, causing the flames near his temples to crackle. "Another?" he asked, holding up the empty pitcher.

Gabriel's face scrunched as if he might snarl in protest, but defeat melted his expression just as quickly. "Might as well pour me a glass of Luce's new whiskey while you're at it."

I squeezed his shoulder and stood. "I gotta run, but don't give up hope just yet. We'll take another stab at the problem in the morning."

I could have gone for some whiskey myself, but I had a feeling there would be plenty of booze served with dinner—social lubricant to warm me to the idea of Tantalus moving in up the river. The thought made my skin crawl.

"Don't forget your jacket," Gabriel said, nodding at the backrest of my abandoned barstool. "Hell's bound to freeze over any day now."

He'd been claiming as much ever since I'd moved in with Bub. I gave Gabriel's curls a ruffle and tugged my jacket on as I headed for the door. Hell freezing sounded like a reasonable next step with the way things were going. But if it meant an end to the raining fire and brimstone smog, who was I to complain?

CHAPTER TEN

"Better to reign in Hell, than to serve in Heaven."
—John Milton, Paradise Lost

Tartarus had been named for a primordial deity overthrown by the Titans long before the First War of Eternity. The territory had originally been located far below Hades' domain, in a dark chasm—an abyss, much like the one Abaddon tended to in the Christian Hell. In fact, what remained of it had been merged with Abaddon's province at the border between the two afterlives, where the land dipped steeply into a valley of shadows before disappearing beyond a black precipice.

Hades had chosen to pay homage to Tartarus by renaming his territory in the treaty drawn up by Grim after the war. The *palace* he shared with Persephone was nestled in the farthest corner of their property, on a ranch surrounded by orchards and fields of asphodel where they raised various livestock. Red mountains bordered the grazing meadows in the distance.

The Egyptian Field of Rushes that marked the border of Aaru stretched on the other side. Which was exactly where I wished I was, rather than seated across from the dreaded goddess of the Greek underworld.

Persephone was three-quarters of the way through a bottle of red wine, but I could still see the erratic throb of her pulse in her delicate neck. Her cheeks flushed any time I looked in her direction as if she expected me to ask her a question she didn't know how to answer. And I'd thought *I* was uncomfortable playing hostess whenever Bub invited his demonic pals over to watch a cricket game.

The goddess's white gown with gold trim was elegant, if a few thousand years out of fashion. It made me feel underdressed in the silky black slip dress that Bub had picked out for me. Hades' black chiton was ancient, too, but it was less obvious alongside Bub's black dress shirt and slacks.

The Lord of the Flies hadn't donned formalwear for quite some time—not since growing out his beard and hair. I expected the tycoon wardrobe and lumberjack grooming to clash, but he was eye-candy as ever. I spent half of dinner mentally picking out clothes for him to model for me once we got home. We needed a date night out to the Hearth soon—a *real* date night that didn't involve deities with agendas.

Persephone licked her grape-stained lips and tilted the bottle of wine toward my glass, offering to fill it as she had each time she'd topped off hers. I shook my head and gave her a strained smile.

"I'd better not," I said, earning a giggle from the goddess.

"I probably shouldn't either, but it's been a long week, and I'm just so glad the construction crew is finally gone."

My stomach knotted as I glanced across the patio to the freshly painted guest house near the swimming pool. It was hard not to be grateful that I hadn't found Tantalus today. As socially awkward as Persephone was, I didn't think I had to worry about another dinner invitation for quite some time.

If they'd been harboring Chef Boyardee, I would've totally lied about washing my hair or having explosive diarrhea or something. The meet-and-greet with his soul on the mortal side would be challenging enough.

At any rate, dinner hadn't been a total bust. No one had offered me an under-the-table bribe, and the food was excellent. The ornate dining table sprawled across the patio belonged in a museum. So did every bowl and platter set between us, overflowing with braised lamb shanks, glazed asparagus, deviled quail eggs, and golden wreaths of braided bread.

Every new dish the veiled nymphs delivered had cued nervous chatter from Persephone. She detailed how each item had either been grown or raised right on the ranch. I cracked a joke about her living life by the seeds of her plants and received a blank stare for my efforts. Agriculture deities had no sense of humor.

Persephone ran out of talking points after dessert had been served and turned her attention to the wine. The silence didn't seem to bother Hades as much, but Bub kept their conversation rolling with his natural charisma. They carried on about some demonic business or other in Pandemonium, leaving Persephone and me to exchange clumsy pleasantries between her guzzling.

Hades chortled at some joke my demon made, and Persephone echoed him with another nervous giggle. She took a hearty swallow from her glass before extending her pinky toward a gooey chocolate lava cake.

"How did you enjoy dessert?" she asked. I took a wild guess that she was about to divulge the origin of every ingredient.

"It was so good," I admitted, mindful of my manners. Insulting goddesses never ended well for anyone.

"Yes, it paired nicely with the wine. Are you sure you wouldn't like another glass?"

"I have to be up early for work," I said, realizing too late that the excuse doubled as a can of worms.

"Speaking of work," Hades cut in suavely, the polar opposite of his anxious wife on the social spectrum, "I hear you're searching for a soul that will hopefully seal up the boundaries of our realm."

I pressed my lips together and nodded. "Yup. That's me."

"We can't thank you enough." Persephone reached across the table and brushed her cool fingers over the top of my hand. "Hecate sent her lampad attendants to stay with us after the last hellcat attack in her grove, but I know they miss their home. The guesthouse had to be redone to accommodate them all."

"You built that for the nymphs?" I swallowed my sigh of relief and tried to feign innocent curiosity. Then my mind caught up with everything else she'd said. "Hellcat attack? There have been hellcat attacks here in Tartarus?" I blinked at Persephone, my heart fluttering with alarm. I knew there were beasts in the abyss and creatures that wandered the wilder outskirts of the hells, but they rarely appeared this close to Hades' palace.

"Only in Hecate's Grove," Hades clarified. "That's where the entrance to our realm used to be, so the border is thinning there first. The hellcats were using it to slip through to the mortal side. It's almost as if someone were summoning them." He paused and smiled sheepishly at my horror. "Don't worry. Cerberus is keeping watch over the grove now."

"I wonder if Hell and Jahannam have found the cracks in their borders yet," Bub mused aloud, sending another wave of nauseating panic through me. The lava cake had turned to cement in my stomach. I was suddenly glad I'd refused a second glass of wine.

"We're so lucky to have you." Persephone gave me a grape-stained smile and patted the top of my hand again. "I wasn't particularly keen on hosting a soul as dark as Tantalus, but once Hecate's lampads can return to the grove, the guesthouse will work perfectly."

Hades tipped his glass of wine in my direction, a silent toast of agreement. "It's practically fate."

CHAPTER ELEVEN

"If you age with somebody, you go through so many roles - you're lovers, friends, enemies, colleagues, strangers; you're brother and sister. That's what intimacy is, if you're with your soulmate."
—Cate Blanchett

UNLIKE THE PROPERTY AROUND the manor, Hades' palace was a good three miles from the nearest coin-travel zone. A luxury chariot driven by a pair of black horses had been sent to pick us up, a veiled lampad at the reins. The same chariot took us back to the gate after we'd said our goodbyes.

I waited until Bub and I had coined back to our front yard before having my meltdown.

"Did you know about the hellcat attacks?" I demanded, kicking my heels off the second we reached the stone steps leading up to our front door.

"Vaguely," he admitted, offering his arm for balance as I rubbed my aching toes. "A lampad at the farmers market last week mentioned a hellcat crashing one of their parties in the grove. I didn't think much of it at the time. It's a rare occurrence but not entirely unheard of."

"And you didn't think to say anything to me about it?" I snatched my hand away from him to gather up my shoes by their stabby, stiletto ends.

Bub grumbled under his breath. "You were already uptight about tonight's dinner. I didn't want to make things worse."

I huffed and stalked off ahead of him, climbing the stone steps to the porch. Rupert opened the front door. His eyes widened at my skewed expression, and he pressed his back against the foyer wall as if trying to blend in with it as I stormed inside.

"Maybe we should consult the Pythia and see if she's had any visions about where Tantalus might be found," Bub suggested as soon as he caught up to me in the living room. I spun around and pointed my shoes at him.

"Absolutely not. It's December. She's more Maenad than oracle right now."

"Then talk to Morgan," he said, opening his hands as if it were that simple.

"That's not an option either."

"It's not about restoring the throne anymore—"

"I know," I hissed. Rupert peeked around the corner but darted back out of sight at my tone. I wouldn't have thought twice about having this discussion in front of

Jack, but our new butler was still adjusting to Bub's ire. He didn't need mine right now, too.

"I know," I repeated more evenly before heading for the staircase that led to our bedroom. Bub followed a few careful steps behind. He wasn't done with me yet.

"You do know what happens if Hell is unleashed on the mortals, don't you, love?"

"Why, are you going to demon-splain the apocalypse to me?" I glared at him over my shoulder and ducked inside my walk-in closet. Bub stopped in the doorway, leaning against the jamb as he watched me undress.

"I just think you should understand the risks of your hesitation," he said casually as if he weren't accusing me of wanting to watch the world burn.

"Hesitation?" I wadded up the silk dress and threw it in his face. "I sought out every soul on the Fates' list today! I danced and sang and acted like a complete ass to satisfy Hecate—who they clearly sent to supervise rather than assist, seeing as how not even her witches can see her without doing the midnight hokey pokey and turning themselves around their altars. So don't preach at me about *hesitation*, mister."

"You're doing exactly what's expected of you. No less, but certainly no more," he countered, pausing to hook the expensive dress over a hanger. "If you really care about solving this, you should be seeking assistance from your most knowledgeable allies—like Morgan."

"I can't go to Morgan," I insisted, throwing my arms wide. Standing in nothing but my lacy undergarments made it sound more as if I were complaining about having nothing to wear.

"And why not?" Bub's brow scrunched in confusion. "You saved her life—her soul. Is a little advice too much to expect in return?"

"I can't go to Morgan because it would violate the terms of my sworn boon to Una," I confessed. "Do you remember the deal I struck with the faerie queen the night Winston and I rescued you from the rebels?"

Bub swallowed but nodded his head. "I hadn't realized you'd fulfilled your favor to her yet."

"It was right after Grim attacked the throne realm. I was only able to save Naledi and Morgan." My breath quivered at the memory of the carnage. "When I took Morgan back to the faerie coast off the Sea of Avalon where she'd be safer, Una said that we were even so long as I never returned."

"I see." Bub's jaw flexed, and he snatched a wool coat from his closet. "Well, I made no such promise. If Una can't be arsed with you, she can have a kerfuffle with me until she sees reason."

"You're leaving now?" I opened my arms again, my racy underthings spelling out a completely different complaint this time. Bub gave me an appreciative once-over even as he tsked.

"There will be time for all that after you save Eternity." He pressed a chaste kiss to my forehead and then slipped out of the room, where I couldn't follow unless I wanted to give poor Rupert heart failure.

I reached for my robe. If I were quick, there was a chance I could stop him before he reached the coin zone out front. But then a better idea came to mind. I grabbed a pair of jeans and a pullover sweater instead.

Bub was right. I could be doing more.

Not that he'd like my idea of what *more* entailed, but beggars couldn't be choosers.

Tasha Henry split her time between a haunted beach house in Miami and a memorial park in the Bahamas. Not as low-key as I would have played things had I been on the lam, but she was sneaky enough to pull it off. It was also how she'd reconnected with me after going underground when Grim went on his killing spree.

There had only been a few sightings, but they were always somewhere near the Gulf of Mexico or the Caribbean Sea. Anytime a harvest found its way onto my docket for one of those regions, I sent Kevin and Eliza off on their own to do a morgue roundup. A hurricane salvage finally put Tasha back on my map. I'd been dropping off care packages ever since.

When I arrived, she was dozing in a poolside lounge chair. The underwater lights glowed a haunting blue and sent dancing shadows over the entire patio. A fluffy pair of black cats sprawled over Tasha's chest and stomach, purring in time with her snores. My sudden appearance sent them into an alarmed frenzy, hissing and snorting as they clawed their way out of the nap mound and into the pampas grass surrounding the patio.

"*Uhhhh*," Tasha groaned as she inspected the damage to her rag of a band tee shirt.

"Sorry." I grinned innocently. "Isn't that distressed look all the rage right now?"

"Fuck you." Tasha rolled her eyes and lifted the shirt to check how well her stomach had fared after the kitty exodus. A deep scratch above her navel oozed blood. More stained her shirt. "Wonderful."

"I'll bring you some fresh clothes next week," I promised.

There hadn't been much time for planning, but I'd at least stuffed a few bags with nonperishables from the pantry—cuing a panic attack from Rupert. He'd be making an extra trip to the grocery store soon.

Tasha stood and accepted the bags from me. She dumped them onto the counter of a tiki bar sandwiched between an outdoor shower and a hot tub and began taking inventory, sorting the canned goods and boxes onto the empty shelves behind the bar. The homeowners were likely gone for the season, back to whatever big-city job afforded them the summer getaway.

"Prunes? Really?" Tasha made a face at the box and tossed it into the pampas grass, cuing another round of startled noises from the kitties.

"I don't know how those got in there," I said, wondering if Rupert's fussing was more about me hijacking *his* snacks—unless Bub had a dried fruit habit that I was unaware of. "So, how are things?" I asked, changing the subject like a normal person before casually adding, "Come across any hellcats on this side lately?"

Tasha turned to gape at me, a candy bar hanging like a cigar from one side of her mouth. She had another clutched in her hand, but she stuffed it into her back pocket and bit off the end of the one she'd been trying to inhale before swallowing hard.

"Why? Do you see one out there?" She shot a nervous glance at the dark beach in the distance.

I shook my head, trying to soothe her anxiety. "No, I just meant—"

"Then what kind of fucked-up question was that?" she snapped.

"So you *have* seen them." My heart kicked with dreadful anticipation. "The Guard is trying to eradicate the hellcats on the mortal side. The beasts have been slipping through gaps in the fringes of several under-world territories. It's becoming a real problem. The nephilim have suffered dozens of casualties, and we even lost two reapers today."

Tasha was clearly spooked, but she brushed it off as she did most things—with a shrug and a snide remark. "You wanted to make an omelet. Behold, the broken eggs." She stuffed the half-eaten candy bar into her mouth and turned back to the dry goods.

"I don't regret breaking the throne," I said defensively. "I'm only sharing this information with you because I thought it might be useful. This could be your chance to petition for a pardon. Reapers Inc. is in desperate need right now."

Tasha snorted. "Are we talking about the Reapers Inc. run by the backstabbing bitch who offered me a pretend pardon the last time I helped out?"

"That was different." I grimaced, not fully believing the claim myself. "Jenni didn't do that out of spite. She tried to convince the council to exonerate you."

"But she didn't help you bust me out, did she?" Tasha finished her sorting and folded her arms over the tiki counter. Her lethal gaze bore into mine, daring me to lie to her. I needed a different angle.

"Look…" I rested my hands on the back of a barstool and lowered my voice. The dead had ears—and, theoretically, even some of the living could hear me.

"The council has me searching for original believers again," I confessed, drawing a gasp from Tasha.

"You're going to restore the throne?"

"No, they think installing resident sinners in the breached afterlives will fortify the borders. That's the council's Hail Mary plan, anyway. They have me working with Hecate. The Fates gave her permission to off the three chosen original believers early."

"Whoa." Tasha blew out a stiff breath. "That *is* serious. Which souls are you hunting?"

"Judas, Zaynab, and Tantalus."

"Good luck with that, precious. They all sound like demon bait."

"I could really use your help," I said.

"No, what you could use is a grenade launcher." Tasha cackled dryly, but then the humor melted from her expression. "These hellcats…they're not the cute, fluffy kind that Caim and Seth played fetch with. They're bigger and louder. Like dragons with lion heads."

That was the second mention of hellcats that looked like lions. I filed the detail in the back of my mind for later and refocused my attention, doubling down on my current objective.

"So, you have experience with them. All the more reason you should help. We could take your petition directly to the council this time," I offered. "Demand that they publicly acknowledge your pardon first."

She loosed a grumbling sigh. "What makes you think I want to go back to Limbo City?"

"Come on, Tash." I waved my hands around the patio. "Are you honestly enjoying *this*? I know you're not exactly a people person, but don't you ever get lonely?"

The corners of her eyes pinched, and I worried that I had struck a nerve. But she recovered quickly with a sad smile.

"I may get lonely, precious, but at least I'm free."

CHAPTER TWELVE

"What after all, is a halo?
It's only one more thing to keep clean."
—Christopher Fry

I WASN'T SURPRISED THAT BUB wasn't home when I returned from my visit with Tasha. When the Prince of Demons threatened a kerfuffle, he meant it. And Una would not be an easy audience to sway, no matter how thick my demon laid on the charm or intimidation.

Still, it made for a restless night of tossing and turning, even with two freshly groomed hellhounds warming my feet. They'd forgiven me for the backyard quarantine, but I received an ankle nip or two for my fidgety bed etiquette. The few hours of sleep I managed—in the wee hours of the morning—got ruined by a nightmare where I was trapped in a lion enclosure at a zoo after hours.

I woke up with a scream in my throat but swallowed it when I noticed Bub lying beside me. His black dress shirt and slacks were in a pile on the floor as if he'd barely had the energy to strip out of them before falling into bed. I'd save my questions for tonight when I would, hopefully, have good news to share.

The hunt was bound to go better today. After providing us with a list of eighteen useless souls, the Fates' reputation was at stake. They were a proud trio, and they had more to lose than most if Eternity fell apart. They would try harder when curating the list for today.

Of course, better soul candidates meant a better chance of encountering hellcats—lion-faced or otherwise—and whoever was possibly summoning them if Hades' theory was correct. Which meant I was in need of a demon expert.

I dressed in a hurry and rushed through my morning, feeding the hounds and sucking down a cup of piping-hot coffee between apologizing to Rupert for raiding his snack stash. He insisted that he didn't mind, but I suspected the coffee was extra strong because of the longer day he would now have running errands in the city.

I left before Bub woke, coining off to the harbor, where I repeated the donuts and docket review with Kevin and Eliza. Luckily, they were fully clothed when I arrived this time.

"These are all low-risk souls, and they're in Posy lots," Kevin said, scanning the list I'd transferred from my docket to his. I hated to be the one to break the news, but my apprentices deserved to hear it from me rather than the *Daily Reaper Report*, or worse, *Limbo's Laundry*.

"Arden needs extra help right now," I said. "Molly Driver and her apprentice were killed in the line of duty yesterday."

Eliza sucked in a sharp breath. "Hellcats?"

"Maybe. They're not entirely sure," I confessed. "When Special Ops is officially reinstated, we'll likely be working alongside the Posies again to help with their recent surplus of souls. If they want me to keep searching for original believers, that would be the most logical move."

Kevin waved his docket at me. "We could push these a day without any repercussions."

"I'm okay with playing catchup tomorrow," Eliza added.

"I know, I know." I opened the donut box, literally sugarcoating my apology. "I wish it were up to me, but it's not," I said as Kevin grabbed another chocolate Danish. I'd splurged on the deluxe assortment, anticipating this conversation. "Besides, there's a chance you'll receive an extra soul or two this afternoon once Regina divvies up the rest of Molly's list."

"We should be with you." Eliza's voice hitched with concern. "The souls you're after are the worst of the worst. I bet they reek of the underworld. The demons loose on the mortal side will be attracted to them."

"For real," Kevin agreed around a mouthful of pastry. "I know you have Gabriel, but do you really trust Hecate to have your back? As well as we would?"

"I'd love to have you with me on this assignment—both of you—but like I keep saying, it's not up to me." I shrugged and set the donut box on the hatch platform before backing toward the ramp. Saul and Coreen trotted alongside me, tongues lolling and tails wagging. "I'll ask Jenni again, but with as shorthanded as she is, I won't force the issue."

Kevin and Eliza scowled, their displeasure with the situation on full display. I didn't like it either, though I was glad that I didn't have to worry about getting them killed on the job. Low-risk Posy harvests were boring, but at least they'd be safe.

I took the ramp down to the dock pier and coined off to knock out a handful of harvests. I wasn't jerk enough to leave my apprentices with the entire workload, but my list was shorter today. I had two extra stops to make before meeting with Jenni again.

I'd chosen several medium-risk hell-bounds for myself. Not an ideal lot, but I wouldn't have sent Kevin and Eliza out to collect them on their own, even if the mortal side hadn't been infested with hellcats. My senses remained on high alert all morning, searching every shadow for movement. The hounds took notice and remained vigilant, as well. They widened our working perimeter, ears perked and noses in the air, sniffing for hints of brimstone.

After we shuffled the last of my catches back to the harbor and secured them in the hold, I ordered the hounds to keep watch until I returned to collect them for the soul hunt. Then I ditched my robe and headed into the city.

Limbo was peaceful mid-morning, the reapers, nephilim, and factory souls all hard at work. Only a handful of lesser celestials and infernals wandered the streets, window-shopping or jogging. Tent signs littered the sidewalk, advertising brunch specials and holiday sales. A light breeze spread the warm, sugar-cinnamon fragrance of chestnuts from a vendor cart. I shot it a longing glance as I hurried by and silently promised myself a treat if the search was successful today. Of course, half of that depended on the Fates' archives and how reliable they were. The other half of my concern was the reason I'd made time to visit the Reaper Academy.

When Cindy Morningstar had ordered Beelzebub to go undercover with the rebels, she'd also ordered him not to reveal the ruse to anyone—not the Afterlife Council, not me, and not even his most faithful servant: Jackson Bifrons Leonard Melchom.

Jack had been so much more than a butler. He did everything for the Lord of the Flies, and so intuitively that it was a wonder he hadn't guessed the truth of the situation before it was too late. Once the news had broken that Beelzebub was a traitor working for Seth, they'd frozen his assets, and the manor was ransacked and burned to the ground.

Maalik and I had arrived in time to rescue Jack from the worst of it, but only after he'd suffered a serious crack in one of his horns. We'd taken him to Meng's to be treated, and it was at her temple in the woods along the southern coast of Limbo City where Jack began to build a new life for himself—one with romance and public prestige.

He'd helped Meng build the infirmary alongside her temple, tending the sickbeds while warming hers. He also worked part-time at the academy, teaching courses on demon defense and infernal history. His butler days were over. There was no time for planning demonic soirees or washing the Prince of Demons' undies.

On Fridays, Jack graded papers in his office at the academy—or napped, as I caught him doing today. I supposed he didn't get much rest around the temple or the infirmary. As hard as he'd worked for Bub, there had been more leisure time between his duties at the manor, and none of his tasks had been as demanding as tending to nephilim with broken wings or reapers with hellcat bites.

The old demon's horns were tilted up at the ceiling. His head rested on the back of his chair, and thunder rattled from his nostrils, though the hand on his desk gripped a red ink pen. I gently rapped my knuckles against the doorframe.

"What? Who?" Jack stammered, coming to with a startled grunt before catching sight of me. "Oh, Lana! I didn't see you there."

"I don't see much with my eyes closed either," I said, grinning as his face flushed.

"I was just resting my eyes for a moment." He shuffled a stack of papers on his desk and pushed his reading glasses up the bridge of his nose. "All this grading is a strain on them, you know."

"Naturally."

"How's Rupert working out?" Jack asked, steering the conversation away from his embarrassment. "Is he a better fit than my last referral?"

"He's great—well, he's not you, obviously. It's the one thing Bub can't seem to forgive them for."

"Don't tell me the old boy is still on about all that." Jack gave me a knowing grin, but he changed the subject before I could divulge just how *on about all that* Bub really was. "I suppose Jenni has informed you that I'll be delivering the regression tea in Meng's stead." At my surprise, he added, "It's far too dangerous, and I'm better versed in the hell regions where the service is required."

"Right, of course," I said. "Actually, I'm here about something else."

"Do tell."

"I'm having trouble identifying a creature."

"Did you get a good look at it?" Jack asked.

"I haven't witnessed it personally, but there have been several accounts of hellcats, or rather beasts similar to hellcats that look more like lions."

"Do they bear any marks or sigils? Claws or talons? Anything special about their tails?"

"Uh…" I chewed my bottom lip. "Sorry, the lion faces are all I've got. Any ideas?"

Jack frowned, but he stood and went to a bookshelf in the corner of his office. "Hard to say for certain with so little to go on, but taking the potential apocalypse into consideration, there are several possibilities." His fingers skimmed the titles of the old volumes until he found the one he was looking for and plucked the crusty tome from the shelf. The leather spine was so brittle that bits of it crumbled and fell off as Jack laid the book on his desk and opened the front cover. My Latin was rusty, but I stumbled through it at the demon's prodding.

"*Finis Omnis Vitae et Mortis.* The End of All Life and Death?"

"Yes, very dark reading, as you can imagine." Jack turned the page delicately and squinted at the book's table of contents before skipping ahead. "There are so many various eschatological theories, second comings and final judgments, but I think I can at least give you a few things to look for if you encounter one of these beasts personally."

"If I survive long enough to take field notes on the thing," I said under my breath. The idea of coming face-to-face with whatever had taken out thirty of Ross's guards and Molly Driver, a reaper four hundred years my senior, was not part of the plan. But it was best to be prepared.

"Let's see…" Jack thumbed ahead to an illustrated page of average-looking lions, none of which I thought anyone would ever mistake for a hellcat. "There's the Christian Armageddon that details four living creatures, the first having the face of a lion. But then there's also the winged Lion of Saint Mark, and the Lion of Judah—which sometimes appears as a lamb."

"But aren't those divine beings?" I asked. "Why would they attack the Nephilim Guard?"

Jack eyed me over the rim of his glasses. A gently patronizing smile curled the corners of his mouth. "You forget that the offspring of the fallen have not always enjoyed such freedom or respect in Eternity. As soulless beings with an outcast lineage, they are still susceptible to the wrath of Heaven if left at its mercy."

Eternity's history was just as riddled with embarrassing follies as the mortal side. It was easy to forget sometimes, but the gods had been made in humanity's image, and as such, they reflected their biases and cruelty, their elitism and greed.

"But as far as demons go"—Jack turned to another page, revealing a lion-faced creature with a scorpion stinger for a tail—"we have Abaddon's locusts from the abyss"—he turned the page again, this time to a full spread of an even larger beast with a bushy mane and a snapping snake head in place of its tail—"and about two hundred million of these pretties said to be summoned by the four angels bound at the banks of the Euphrates."

"Two hundred million, you say?" My tongue was suddenly dry, and I could feel my pulse vibrating in my eye sockets. "Gabriel said something about a falling star and a key…"

"Yes, well, a fallen star is a whimsical euphemism for so many things. Regardless, the abyss was quite secure, last I checked," Jack said. "The Euphrates, too."

I swallowed the lump building in the back of my throat. "The Euphrates? Is that the river drying up over in Syria and Iraq?"

"A-plus in geography, young reaper." Jack flipped a few pages ahead in the book. "That's not even your territory. I'm impressed, but you did score well on your L&L."

My gaze shot up from the book of doomsday creatures. "You looked at my transcript?"

"I was curious." He paused to give me another paternal smile. "I wanted to see if you'd always been a difficult pupil or if demon defense just wasn't your forte."

"Hey, I was a good student. It was *Latin* that wasn't my forte."

"True," Jack agreed, turning his attention back to the book. "Regarding the Euphrates River, a handful of deities from Ancient Mesopotamia have lion steeds, though many of them have not been seen since before the First War when they were defeated, and their territories dissolved. Some were killed and had no followers to resurrect them, but a few opted to join the mortal coil—at least, for a time. I believe you met one several winters back."

"Odin," I grumbled, recalling my freezing walk through the snow with Gabriel after getting shafted by a Santa imposter.

"Oh!" Jack stabbed a finger at the next page. "Sekhmet, the lioness-headed Egyptian warrior goddess. The Lady of Slaughter, also known as She Who Mauls. If we're dealing with a singular creature—in addition to the hellcats, of course—then my coin is on her. She comes with an easy solution, as well. It's said that Ra fed her red-dyed beer to sate her bloodlust."

"Beer makes everything better," I said, wondering if Jenni would go for such a plan. She'd probably want to confirm that Sekhmet had gone AWOL first and that I wasn't just trying to be sneaky about drinking on the job.

"I'll keep digging," Jack offered. "But knowing more about this beast would certainly help. Please, do share any new details you discover."

"Thanks, Jack." I tilted my head to one side, laying it on his shoulder as he wrapped an arm around my back and gave me a squeeze. "I appreciate you doing this."

"Just don't tell Master Beelzebub," he whispered as if a tiny, winged spy might be eavesdropping. I grinned at his use of *master*. Bub hadn't been his master for some time now, but old habits die hard—especially habits that were hundreds of years old.

"I better take off," I said, easing toward the exit as Jack fetched another volume from his shelf.

"Happy hunting," he called after me. "Fates willing, I'll be there to celebrate your victory upon your return."

"Fates willing," I echoed, ignoring the coil of dread squeezing my insides.

CHAPTER THIRTEEN

"The awakening of the soul to its bondage and its effort to stand up and assert itself – this is called life."
—*Swami Vivekananda*

My second errand before convening with Jenni and the soul-searching party took me back to the seventy-first floor of the Reapers Inc. building. My retractable scythe was fixed and ready to be picked up. And despite my recent proximity with an unhealthy amount of demon bait, I'd managed to keep Warren's loaner scythe in one piece.

While it was true that the weapon had been designed more for show than battle, it was at least *somewhat* effective in combat. I'd tested the limits of that theory more times than I'd ever actually admit to Warren. Still, my mounting anxiety wouldn't allow me to rely solely on a weapon that had fallen apart almost as often as it had saved me. I couldn't appear to an original believer with my battle axe strapped across my back, but that didn't mean my boots weren't stuffed with knives and my pockets with throwing stars and cans of angelica mace.

Regardless, it sure felt good showing up at Warren's with a scythe that wasn't busted and leaving with mine strapped to my hip—especially with the reinforced titanium hinge that Lindy had installed. Maybe the squeaky wheel got the grease, but the one that broke all the damn time got the premium upgrades.

I bumped into Gabriel in the elevator on the way up to Jenni's office. The circles under his eyes spelled out how the rest of his evening had gone after we'd parted ways at Purgatory Lounge, and a small twinge of guilt wormed its way into my heart.

"I'm sure Regina has fresh coffee in the break room," I offered in lieu of a proper greeting. Gabriel grunted in reply. "Was that *thanks* or *fuck off*?" I asked.

"Both," he said, his bloodshot gaze too tired to meet mine.

"Fair enough."

Before my move to the underworld, a hard night out would have ended with one of us crashing on the other's couch, John Wayne playing in the background. Work had been extra grueling these past few years, and I hadn't found time for much more than an occasional drink or two before coining home. Even our poker nights had been cut back to once a month.

The elevator opened on the Reapers Inc. lobby in time for Gabriel and me to witness Regina's clumsy retreat from Jenni's closed office door. The nephilim secretary flopped onto the edge of her chair so hard that she nearly rolled into a filing cabinet. Her wings fluttered, and her hands slapped at the top of her desk, halting her trajectory.

"Good morning, welcome to Reapers Inc.," Regina blurted, then realized it was only us. "President Fang is in a meeting—"

"Did it take pressing your ear against her door to figure that one out?" I smirked, enjoying the way her face turned as red as her springy curls. "Well, the whole point of eavesdropping is to collect gossip fodder, so out with it. Who's the boss entertaining in there?"

Regina opened her mouth, quickly closing it again before any words escaped. I couldn't quite tell if she was afraid of being fired for spilling the beans or if she just didn't know the answer.

"Give her a break." Gabriel paused to yawn into his closed fist. "We'll find out soon enough," he added at my scowl. "Didn't you say something about coffee?"

"Do you take cream or sugar?" Regina asked, popping up from her chair. Her infomercial smile returned with a vengeance, but I resisted the urge to bug-eye her teeth as if she had spinach stuck between them.

"Lots and lots," Gabriel answered as he followed her down the back hall toward the break room. Regina's bubbly giggle grated on my nerves, but her fangirling over an archangel was typical. The nephilim were off-spring of the fallen, though most tended to emphasize their relation to the heavenly hosts in good standing. Not that any amount of sucking up would get them into Heaven. They were stuck in Limbo, same as the reapers.

The slow ticking of the clock on the wall behind the front desk was louder without anyone else around to fill the silence. I shot a suspicious glance at Jenni's office door. As I contemplated testing my luck in the same fashion Regina had, it opened, and a middle-aged female soul exited, quietly closing the door behind her. My breath hitched as her gaze locked with mine, and my heart suddenly became trapped in my throat.

There was nothing especially unique about her floral print skirt or the matronly bun at the nape of her neck. Yet, I felt the tug of familiarity. Had I harvested this woman? Was she a factory soul that I'd smuggled away from the sea and to the Fates for employment? I couldn't place her, and it bothered me.

The woman smiled as if she recognized me, as well. It wasn't a reaction I was used to from souls—especially if I happened to be the one who had collected them after they'd expired. She crossed the lobby with a purposeful stride, and for a second, I thought she might attempt to hug me. Thankfully, she extended a hand instead. I shook it, ignoring the zap of static electricity when we touched.

"I wondered when we'd finally meet," she said, her smile stretching wider. "Cordelia Murni, ambassador for the Woke Souls."

"Woke Souls?" I echoed. "You mean the ones on the Isles of Eternity?"

"Yes. And I must say, we're all very curious about you." She lowered her voice before continuing. "The council has been quite secretive regarding your involvement with our founding, but we know who deserves our respect and gratitude. Speaking of which, you should come to our winter festival tomorrow evening."

My face warmed at the invitation, but the political implications kept my head from floating off into the clouds. "I don't know if President Fang would approve—"

"President Fang holds no dominion over our territory, and neither does the council," Cordelia said, her voice taking on a sharp edge. "*We* decide who is allowed on the isles."

"Okay." I couldn't bring myself to refuse the offer a second time. It was too monumental. As far as I knew, they'd never invited anyone else to visit the mysterious community on the isles.

Cordelia's smile returned at my acceptance. "Wonderful." She reached past me and pressed a button to call an elevator. "Tomorrow, at twilight. Beach your watercraft on the east coast of the northernmost isle," she instructed. "Someone will be waiting to lead you into the village."

"Twilight, east coast, northern isle," I repeated, making a mental note to charge the battery on one of the ship's electric tenders in the morning.

The phone on the front desk beeped, and voices echoed from the back hallway as an elevator opened. Cordelia nodded in farewell and slipped inside. The doors closed just as Gabriel and Regina reappeared in the lobby. The nephilim peeled her eyes away from Gabriel and frowned up at the glowing light above the stainless-steel doors, but before she could question it, a second set slid open, revealing Hecate.

The goddess looked from Gabriel to me and pursed her lips as if she didn't care for being the last to arrive. A long, wool cloak hung around her shoulders. It was somehow both archaic and fashionable paired with the dark pantsuit she wore beneath.

"You look…cozy," I said, noting the earmuffs and leather gloves that completed her outfit.

Hecate shrugged. "The Fates mentioned there might be an extra chilly stop or two for today."

"Thanks for the heads-up." Gabriel snorted and slurped his cup of coffee. I hoped it would improve his mood soon, but more than that, I hoped it sharpened his focus. I needed him on his A-game if we encountered demons.

Jenni poked her head out of her office. She glared at the flashing intercom light on Regina's desk before addressing the rest of us. "Let's get this over with," she grumbled.

Gabriel's wings fluffed in offense at her tone, and several feathers dropped to the lobby floor as he followed Hecate inside the office. I brought up the rear, earning an extra dose of Jenni's irritation as she waved an arm to hurry me along.

I was too distracted to be insulted. But, considering the surplus of sourpusses, I decided that now probably wasn't the best time to gloat about my exclusive invite.

I'd save that for after the party.

CHAPTER FOURTEEN

"I asked God for a bike, but I know God doesn't
work that way. So I stole a bike and asked for forgiveness."
—*Emo Philips*

IT WAS HARD NOT TO GET my hopes up after the chance encounter with Cordelia. But in my experience, good luck never seemed to last long.

The eighteen candidates on the Fates' new list were more scattered than the first set had been, taking us from South Africa to New Zealand, France to Ireland, Wales to Siberia. The temperature and humidity shifts were murder on my curls, and my leather jacket was no match for the teeth-chattering, lip-chapping winds blowing down from the Urals, but I dared not complain with Gabriel in thin linen and sandals.

The hounds whimpered their discontent, and even our exiled mark looked miserable in his fur-lined hat and thick down coat. I screamed and danced a circle around him in the spitting snow, testing his spiritual vision with asinine zeal so that Hecate had no reason to demand a second attempt. Her shivering nod of approval came before I'd even finished. It had taken thirty minutes to track the man down—long enough to make even a goddess fret over frostbite.

I saved the souls in the United States for last, four of which were in Salem, Massachusetts. Hecate didn't voice her displeasure so much as she let the whip and snap of her cloak express her frustration at being given low priority.

Khadija remained at the forefront of my mind. But in the end, it didn't really matter.

By the time we reached our last stop, we hadn't collected a single original believer.

The Texas sun hung low in the sky, easing the chill that hadn't left my bones since Russia. Cape Town and Auckland had been warmer, but the damp cold of Europe followed, leading to our trek across the Siberian tundra. There was a hot bath in my future—plus wine and probably some whining. The day was shaping up to be another bust.

"Quo fata ferunt," Hecate hissed. Wither the Fates carry us. Laced with sarcasm, the Latin motto sounded more like a curse. The goddess stripped off her cloak and draped it over one arm before yanking off her gloves and earmuffs.

I turned in a slow circle, realizing we'd manifested in a parking lot. Thousands of lined spaces stretched into the distance. At least we'd been deposited near the building they belonged to—a megachurch that looked large enough to host the Olympics.

"Ugh, prosperity preachers are the *worst*." Gabriel groaned and leaned against a red sports car. He kicked off a sandal and rubbed his heel as he glared up at the structure. "What sort of demented game are the Fates playing with us? It's going to take forever to find him in there."

"Not necessarily," I said, skimming the digital file on my docket. "Scooter Stone should be heading out any minute now."

"So, we can just jump him before he gets to his car?" Gabriel asked as if we were street thugs planning a grand theft auto heist. He glanced around at the shiny trucks and luxury cars that filled the lot. "Which one is his?"

"You're sitting on it," I answered after double-checking the license plate.

"I should have known." Gabriel gave the red two-seater a once-over and rolled his eyes. "'Woe unto you that are rich, for ye have received your consolation.' I'm guessing this one is a Judas candidate?"

"Most likely." I frowned, annoyed that the Fates had left that particular detail off each file again. However, they managed to include a note about the recent vacation that Pastor Stone had taken on his private yacht.

Maybe the Fates expected his Caribbean tan to stand out and make him more recognizable. Either that or they wanted to make sure I knew how he spent the money that he'd conned his followers out of, many of whom he'd convinced would be blessed with infinite wealth so long as they donated their last dollar to his so-called *church*. As if this information might make me feel less guilty about collecting his soul ahead of schedule.

Honestly, it kind of did.

Saul sniffed the sports car's bumper. Then he released a soft *woof*, licked the back of my hand, and pointed his nose toward the building. Someone was emerging from the long shadow it cast over the parking lot.

"Here we go," I said, eager for the day to be over, one way or another.

The man matched the press release photo in his file, from the expensive suit to the over-moussed hair. As expected, his complexion was more sun-kissed than in the picture, though his hair was a shade darker. Unnaturally white teeth gleamed as he spoke into the cell phone pressed to his ear.

"I think Gloria went a little overboard touching up the grays this time," he said with an arrogant drawl. "Get rid of her. Find me someone else—someone younger with a tight ass."

I wondered if that request made it into his bedtime prayers. *Bless the poor fools I've robbed blind, and send me a juicier stylist for my next extramarital fling.*

The conversation made Gabriel cringe, too. "If he's another dud, we should at least let the hellhounds take a dump on his leather seats before we go," the angel said.

Hecate's eyebrows arched as if the idea amused her. "Then we'd better hurry. You're up, Lana." She nodded at our mark, cuing my pulse to kick in my throat.

My nerves were less twitchy today, but that was mostly because they were shot from all the disappointment. Still, the humiliating jackass improv worked up an uncomfortable sweat. Hecate wasn't satisfied unless my efforts were absurd enough to startle a guard outside Buckingham Palace.

I stepped between Scooter and his car and did a little boot-slap dance, punctuating the end with a jumping jack and a rodeo-quality, "Yeehaw!"

Scooter said goodbye to whoever was responsible for fulfilling his vulgar wishes and slipped his phone into the breast pocket of his suit jacket. I was about to engage in act two of my invisible performance when he amped up the wattage on his smile.

"Sorry, miss, but the book signing was this morning. I'm all out of time for autographs."

"You can see me?" I sucked in a surprised breath and did another jumping jack—in celebration this time. "He can see me!"

"Hallelujah!" Gabriel whooped and did a dance of his own, his wings lifting him into the air. He landed beside me and rubbed his hands together.

"Well, of course," Scooter cooed, his gaze dropping briefly to my chest. "I see *all* God's children—every Sunday morning, from nine to eleven on the Blessed by Stone Network."

"Oh, *barf*." I made a face at Hecate. "What happens now? How do we kill him?"

Scooter's gaze narrowed as he looked right through the goddess and then back to me. "Can I call someone for you, miss? A caregiver, maybe? Or the police?"

"This will just take a second," I promised, pressing a hand against his driver's side door as he reached for the handle.

Hecate tossed her cloak and gloves onto the hood of Scooter's car. Overhead, the clouds slowly blotted out the sun, and a cool wind wove through the parking lot. It lifted the goddess's dark locks, fanning them around her head.

Saul and Coreen whimpered and lay down at her feet, placing their muzzles between their paws. Like Anubis, Hecate was a canine deity. She held sway over them and demanded their respect, though the idea of my hounds obeying anyone else, even a goddess, irked me. After all, she wasn't the one forking over half her salary for Cerberus Chow and doggie spa treatments.

Hecate's eyes glowed an eerie blue, the color of the soul auras I'd once been able to see. It tinged the air the way an approaching storm sometimes stained everything green. I wasn't sure if Scooter could see the color, but he certainly noticed the wind. It was playing hell on his meticulously groomed hair.

The cluster of key charms hanging around Hecate's neck chimed, playing an eldritch tune that drew Gabriel's attention away from our mark. The angel's quizzical expression hardened, and he shot me a frown that I didn't understand. His concerns would have to wait.

Hecate unsheathed a dagger from her hip. The dark leather blended in with her slacks, but the silver blade glowed blue like her eyes. She pointed it at Scooter and whispered, *"Mors vincit omnia."*

Death conquers all.

For a split second, I saw the shimmer of his soul beneath the surface of his skin.

"Now," Hecate said. "The spell will not last forever, reaper."

I touched Scooter's arm, and his soul broke free, splashing to the pavement like a burst water balloon. It reformed just as quickly, taking on the earthly shape of his shucked meatsuit. Judas wouldn't emerge until he'd had a cup of Meng's tea. I could at least be thankful for that, though Scooter was no prize in the meantime.

"What the hell have you done to me?" he demanded, his eyes growing three sizes as he took in Gabriel and Hecate, and then his ashen corpse sprawled across the parking lot. "No, no, no," he wailed. "This can't be happening. I'm God's chosen!" He threw his arms over the top of his sports car. "See how He's blessed me?"

"In your sick, twisted dreams." Gabriel scoffed. "'Fool! This night your soul is required of you, and the things you have prepared, whose will they be?'"

"Seriously, Gabe?" I grabbed my hips and stared at him. "Preaching to a hell-bound soul?"

"Hell-bound?" Scooter cried. "There must be some mistake. I'm a man of God."

"So was Judas," Gabriel went on, unable to help himself, "until he traded his soul for thirty pieces of silver. How many pieces of silver did *this* cost you?" he demanded, waving his arm at the megachurch.

"I'll give it all away," Scooter said, petting his sports car as if it were a security blanket.

"It's too late for that." Gabriel reached for the soul but froze at Saul's sudden growl. The angel's gaze migrated to my hound. Saul had been trained to protect my catches, but Gabriel's move didn't seem to be what bothered the hellhound now.

Coreen's ears flattened as she sniffed the air, trying to sense what had set off her brother. And then a diabolic roar sounded in the parking lot behind us.

The sound sent adrenaline splintering through my veins, and my hand instinctively went to my scythe as I envisioned the creatures from Jack's doomsday of all doomsdays book. My head turned slowly, stiff with terror.

In the reflection of a shiny black SUV, I caught a glimpse of movement.

"Get down!" Gabriel shouted, shoving me to the ground as a spear smashed through the windshield of Scooter's car.

"My baby!" Scooter wailed.

Then a mangy hellcat the size of a Clydesdale pounced on the hood. More leather wings whistled overhead. They'd crept in under the cover of Hecate's spell.

The unsettling roar came again, closer this time. It drew a yelp from Scooter. He tore off, running toward the entrance of the megachurch. If he made it inside, we'd have one hell of a time finding him.

I stood and flicked open my scythe, swiping it across the hellcat's throat. The wound was too shallow for an instant death, but it was a maneuver I knew the weapon could survive. And, best of all, it kept the beast from screeching in my face. The blood, on the other hand, was not so easily avoided.

"Perfect," Gabriel snarled as he scrambled away from the car. His white linen outfit was ruined.

"Sorry." I gave him a pained smile and turned to Hecate, but with her black suit, I couldn't tell if she'd escaped the horror-set treatment.

"Go get the soul," she shouted over the flurry of hellcats descending on the parking lot. "We'll hold them off."

Gabriel didn't look thrilled by her plan, but he nodded in agreement and wrenched the spear out of Scooter's windshield before taking flight.

Hecate's eyes turned spooky again, and the wind picked up speed. She sheathed her dagger and knelt between my hounds, stroking their backs until their eyes filled with blue light. I ground my teeth, swallowing my protest as they leapt to their feet and followed her. Her overreaching would have to be addressed, but for now, I had a soul to catch.

I gripped my scythe in both hands and sprinted after Scooter. He hadn't quite reached the entrance to the church, but that was probably because he tripped over his feet every time he looked up at the hellcats circling overhead. If I watched closely, I hoped I'd see which way he went once he made it inside.

Tall, glass doors spread across the front of the building, giving a crystal-clear view of the lavish foyer beyond.

More doors inside led to what I imagined was the arena where Scooter recorded his blasphemous sermons.

Like most souls that refused to accept their deaths, I expected he would try to find someone he knew and yell and scream as if they would hear him if he only tried hard enough. That little one-sided game of Marco Polo had saved my ass more times than I could count.

I was sure it would have saved me this time, too, if Tasha Henry hadn't appeared at the top of the stairs just as Scooter topped them, wheezing and blubbering. She hooked an arm around his neck and jerked him against her body before grinning down at me.

"I'll take it from here, precious," Tasha said. Then she blew me a kiss and rolled her coin, disappearing with my soul.

CHAPTER FIFTEEN

"I'm sure wherever my dad is, he's looking down on us.
He's not dead, just very condescending."
—Jack Whitehall

THERE WAS A VEIN IN Jenni's forehead I had never noticed before. It quivered with each word she forced past
clenched teeth. "What the hell am I supposed to do with
you, Lana?"

My dread was somewhat quelled by visions of her
apartment layered over Grim's old torturing grounds,
but my sense of shame was doing just fine.

"I had no idea she would be there. I swear."

Jenni slammed her fist on her desk, rattling the
blood-spattered spear that Gabriel had presented with
our report. "Now I have to redirect resources we don't
have to spare to infiltrate the ghost market—not that
they'll have enough time before a soul as high-priority as
Judas is sold off. Which means I'll have to send another
team to retrieve the soul once we discover who the buyer
is."

"Special Ops can handle that," I offered, earning a berating laugh from Jenni.

"You don't honestly think the council will approve the new unit after this massive fuck-up, do you? You'll be lucky if they don't demand your head, along with Tasha's."

"Hey, I wasn't the only one on this assignment," I snapped, instantly regretting my outburst when Gabriel and Hecate both turned to glare at me from where they brooded in opposite corners of the room.

"I did everything but prostrate that soul for you," Hecate said, though her cold gaze suggested she would have liked to prostrate *me*.

"Oh, you did plenty, including hijacking my hounds, who would have otherwise aided me in rounding up the soul before Tasha nabbed it."

"*Your* hounds? All dogs are mine to call on by rights of Greek antiquity," she countered, lifting her chin. "If they were truly yours, they'd obey your call over mine."

"If you hadn't used your blue-eyed doggo witchery, they would have." I harumphed and folded my arms.

Gabriel was unusually quiet, but I expected to get an earful from him later, too. He wouldn't criticize me about Tasha in front of Hecate. Jenni, however, had no such objections.

"When I tell the council who has the soul, where do you suppose they'll assign the blame, Lana?" She folded her hands over her desk, lacing her fingers so tightly they turned red. I got the feeling she was imagining them around my neck. "What do you think will happen when Tasha's taken into custody? What might she reveal in exchange for her freedom—freedom that she wouldn't have in the first place if *someone* hadn't helped her escape?"

My tongue felt like sandpaper on the roof of my mouth, but I patted myself on the back for not breaking eye contact with Jenni. There was no proof of my crime. And it had been the right thing to do—a concept that Tasha clearly couldn't wrap her conscience around.

"She's evaded the Nephilim Guard this long," I said, ignoring the accusation. "What makes you think they'll have any better luck finding her now?"

"Because she's a threat." Jenni's unwavering stare bored into mine. "The council didn't care so much when she was just an exiled rebel without a cause. But now, she's put all of Eternity in jeopardy. She's painted a fresh target on her back, and she's already proven that she has no problem stabbing yours to get what she wants."

Boy, had she ever.

The hypothetical interrogations played out like clichéd police dramas in the back of my mind. In every single scenario, Tasha threw me under the bus. Still, she didn't have any more evidence than the council had that I'd helped her. The only credible item that could have counted as proof of my involvement had been Winston's skeleton coin, but Tasha had given that back. I now had it tucked inside a hidden compartment in the heel of my left boot.

Winston had created the coin for his covert outings in Limbo City after the council deactivated coin travel. The travel booths were equipped with cameras, and as the secret soul on the Throne of Eternity, he wasn't exactly in the system. Plus, the throne realm hadn't become a booth destination until after Naledi's debut at the Oracle Ball.

I hadn't used the skeleton coin since the throne had been broken. Part of me worried that its function had dissipated along with the pocket realm made of the same sacred matter. But I also hoped that some trace of the power lingered and that if I only used the coin when absolutely necessary, I could preserve that magic and whatever fragment of Winston's soul was attached to it.

Gabriel's wings fluttered stiffly, dappling the office with reflected light from the window as he turned. At least the hellcat bloodbath had missed his feathers. He crossed the room and nodded down at the spear laid across Jenni's desk.

"I think we may have a bigger problem on our hands than a renegade reaper." He tapped the star-shaped symbol engraved in the stone tied to the spear's shaft. "This could be a sign of the fallen star sent to unlock the abyss and release Abaddon's locusts."

Hecate groaned. "Not this again."

"There was a lion with a scorpion tail," Gabriel insisted. "I saw it with my own eyes."

"There have been no reports from Hell of a breach in the abyss," Jenni said, holding up a hand when he opened his mouth to protest. "I spoke to Abaddon myself, just this morning after a guard at Meng Po's infirmary reported a similar sighting. Whatever the beast is, it's not a locust from Revelation."

"But it *could* be a warning. A vision of what's to come." Gabriel thrust a hand at Hecate. "Was she not once a heavenly being, now fallen to reside in the underworld? The keys to the Greek abyss hang around her neck, and the hellcats plaguing the mortal side are entering through her territory. Are you telling me this is all a coincidence?"

"How dare you?" Hecate hissed. Her eyes tinged with blue light, but somehow it only darkened the shadows pooling at her feet. "My lampads were assaulted, and we've been forced out of our home. My sacred grove was desecrated, and I've even agreed to forsake one of my own followers for this cause. Now, I'm to suffer insults hurled by the *Angel of Ale*?"

"Insults?" Gabriel's chest puffed out defensively. The dried blood across his linen tunic was more ominous paired with his holy outrage. "You're the one who has resorted to name-calling. I've only stated facts, none of which you denied, I noticed."

"Your *facts* are distorted," Hecate said. "I am most certainly *not* fallen. I hold as much sway in Olympus as I do in Tartarus. I simply choose to live in the underworld to keep Persephone company. If anyone is fallen, it's you—off the wagon again, or so I hear."

Jenni covered her face with both hands. This was not how the day was meant to end.

"Hateful hag," Gabriel spat at the goddess, apparently having decided that name-calling wasn't beneath him, after all.

"Booze-bloated pigeon," Hecate replied with equal contempt. The blue fire in her eyes pulsed brighter, and I felt a shift in the air as if my ears might pop.

"*Or*," I interjected before they tried to jumpstart the apocalypse, "I could take the spear to Professor Jackson at the academy and see if he's come across that symbol in his research."

"You want to turn our only lead over to a demon?" Gabriel scoffed.

"Why not?" I hitched an eyebrow, daring him to try me. If he took an unfair shot at Jack, I'd be more than happy to throw Amy in his face. "Jack is far more knowledgeable about these things than most, and I asked him to look into the recent sightings for me."

"Fine," Gabriel snarled. "But the spear's not leaving my sight. I'll take it to him myself."

"Be my guest. Just know that he has a more extensive vocabulary than you do, so I'd take it easy with the verbal abuse."

Jenni pulled her face out of her hands and looked up at us as if she were surprised that we were still in her office. "I have a follow-up council meeting in twenty minutes," she choked out, her voice quivering with dismay.

For a brief window in time, the position Jenni now held as Grim's replacement and the president of Reapers Inc. had almost been mine. I'd turned it down, a decision I still stood by, but most especially at times like these. Being caught between a disgruntled angel and a pissed-off goddess was no picnic. But stuck in a room with a dozen formidable entities who were more often at odds than in agreement?

No thank you.

"Same time tomorrow morning?" I asked, easing out of the guest chair. Jenni stared at me as if I'd grown a second head.

"Have you lost your mind?"

"There are still two other original believers out there." I waved my hand at the window as if they might be walking on the street below. For all we knew, they were. But without my soul vision, I'd never know. And without their mortal bodies, they could see *all* reapers, not just me. It was one hell of a pickle, and no one could deny it was the council's fault we were in it.

"You lost a key soul," Jenni said, reminding me of my own failings.

"We didn't *lose* it." I rolled my eyes. "Tasha stole it—which wouldn't have happened if hellcats hadn't ambushed us or if we'd had a bigger team—"

"Your excuses don't change the outcome." Jenni sighed. "There's no guarantee the Fates would have given us a third list anyway. But the idea of losing another original believer to the ghost market will not sit well with the council. Besides, the Posy Unit is struggling, and now their backlog is overtaxing the Lost Souls Unit. I need you to help them get caught up."

"What about the hellcat attacks and the fractured borders of the underworld?" I asked. "Is that really something we can afford to put on the back burner?"

"There's been talk of relocating Dionysus and his Maenad to Tartarus for the time being," Jenni said, drawing a simultaneous shudder from both Hecate and me. As if the idea of having Tantalus for a neighbor hadn't been cringeworthy enough. "If that fortifies the borders, they could work out a seasonal schedule with Olympus until the council comes up with a better plan of action."

"What about Jahannam?" I swallowed the bile that crept up the back of my throat. "Khadija can't be expected to spend half her time there."

Jenni opened her hands in a helpless gesture. "I suppose that's a problem the council will have to reassess."

"The Fates have to give us another list." I looked from Gabriel to Hecate, hoping they'd back me up. "Right? We can try again, can't we?"

Neither of them seemed overly confident in our ability as a team.

Jenni stood and straightened the lapels of her blazer. She gave the door a pointed look, and I knew she was ready to usher us out so she had a few minutes to compose herself before facing the council. "I'll be in touch," she said dismissively.

"No." I shook my head. "That can't be it." Khadija was counting on me. I didn't care that she couldn't remember who I was to her or who she was to me. I owed her this much. Hell, I owed her everything.

Jenni circled her desk and placed a hand on my shoulder. Her steely gaze creased with sympathy, but her words were firm. "We can only do what we can do, Lana."

I swallowed and gave her a stiff nod, letting her steer me toward the door.

Maybe she was right. But was I doing everything I could?

That was the real question. And once it entered my mind, I couldn't let it go.

CHAPTER SIXTEEN

"Cleanliness becomes more important when godliness is unlikely."
— P. J. O'Rourke

I DIDN'T GO WITH GABRIEL to see Jack. We'd had enough of each other for one day, and I was more concerned with hunting down Tasha than identifying lion-faced demons, which Gabriel couldn't understand with visions of Judgment Day dancing through his head.

To be fair, revenge fantasies were having a rave in mine. I couldn't understand why Tasha would turn on me after everything I'd done for her. And what good was any amount of coin if she was still forced to live on the mortal side where her only companions were disturbed lost souls? I sure as hell wouldn't be bringing her any more care packages—which meant she'd have to rely on someone else. Like maybe her demon ex, Tack.

It was a longshot, but I collected the hounds from the harbor before paying a visit to both of Tasha's hideouts. She was nowhere to be found. Of course. Saul tracked her scent, but it didn't stray far from the perimeter of either property. After a decade of living on the run, she knew how to cover her trail.

I packed up my disappointment and failure and headed home. Rupert was attempting beef Wellington tonight, and I needed to be there to run interference with Bub. Otherwise, we'd be starting over from scratch with a new butler by next week. *If* anyone else was willing to apply for the position.

Thinking of poor Rupert and the extra work I'd already created for him lately, I sequestered the hounds on the back patio after taking the garden hose to them. Their fur was still matted with a fair amount of hellcat blood, but I didn't have the energy to dig out the washtub and Februa suds.

I was surprised not to find Bub in the garden, though the corpse lilies weren't as pungent tonight. Their pollination window must have closed. Maybe we'd be able to enjoy dinner on the patio again soon—so long as the hellcats infesting Hecate's Grove didn't find their way to our backyard.

I kicked off my boots at the back door, then thought better of it and gathered them up so the hounds wouldn't give me a piece of their mind by taking a bite out of my footwear. Coreen grunted in offense, even though I busted her with Bub's Italian Oxfords any time he evicted the hounds from our bed. I gave her a menacing look, which she ignored as she flopped down on the patio beside Saul.

If I'd had Hecate's doggo mojo, hiding my shoes wouldn't have been necessary. I was sure Anubis didn't have to worry about his jackals gnawing on his sandals or taking off with some witchy dog whisperer. Maybe I'd give him a call and see if I could get a trainer or an obedience school recommendation.

I added the task to my list of things to do if the world didn't end and went inside. The smell of roasting potatoes and buttery mushrooms greeted me, and my stomach grumbled happily at the promise of food.

Cooking was not Rupert's strong suit, but against all odds—and the Lord of the Flies' chastising cynicism—he'd improved tremendously over the past few months. The savory aroma lured me into the kitchen, where I found my fussy demon consort at the stove, backseat-cooking over Rupert's shoulder.

"You're burning the Duxelles." Bub scowled at the skillet. "Turn down the heat and add more butter. I swear, you'd think we were torturing souls in the special hell for chefs who try to pass off tilapia as red snapper."

"Does that silver tongue need polishing, demon mine?" I asked, wrapping my arms around his waist and gently tugging him away from the stove. Rupert's shoulders sagged with relief, and the puckered skin around his horns relaxed.

"Welcome home, Lady Lana. Dinner will be ready within the hour," he said, quickly turning his attention back to the stove at Bub's sour expression.

"Thank you, Rupert. I can't wait to try the Wellington."

"Are you sure?" Bub snorted as I ushered him to the opposite side of the long counter that divided the kitchen from the dining room. "It's not too late. I could still pick up a pizza from the nearest Styx Stop."

"We talked about this. You promised you'd save your criticism for after dinner."

"Yes, yes. I know." He leaned down to press his lips to mine and then did a double-take at my hair. "Is that... blood?"

"Maybe." I winced and shot Rupert a hesitant glance. It wasn't so much a matter of not trusting him, but I didn't think his nerves, *or* the beef Wellington, would fare well with the news that the world could be coming to an end.

Bub pulled me closer and dropped his mouth to my ear. "Shall we wash up before dinner?" he whispered, his beard tickling my neck.

If anyone else had been turned on by blood and guts in my hair, I would have called them a freak. But with Beelzebub, it was endearing. He'd explained it once, in the quiet darkness of our bed one night after ravaging me. A vetala, an evil Hindu spirit that liked to possess corpses, had attacked me on the job that afternoon.

Blood in my hair meant there had been a chance that Bub could have lost me. It also meant I'd survived. Maybe he couldn't stand between me and all the dangers I encountered in my line of work, but he could appreciate that I'd fought—and won. That I'd found my way back into his arms again. And he would never take that for granted.

I grinned and let him lead me through the house and up to our bedroom. Rupert would have his peace in the kitchen, and I would have the Prince of Demons' undivided attention. Win-win.

I peeled off my jacket and hung it over the hook inside my closet door. It would need to be properly washed, but I'd wiped off most of the slain hellcat's blood in the bathroom at Reapers Inc. Since white clothing was the ultimate test of Murphy's Law, Gabriel had taken the brunt of the damage. Even so, a thick line of dried blood marred the collar of my sweater. It was ruined.

"Pity," Bub said, touching the blue cashmere. He dug a fingernail in above the stain, and the fabric split open with ease. Hellspawn blood was acidic and had weakened the knit.

"Maybe it can be patched?" I suggested as Bub's fingers widened the hole and traced my collarbone. His lips brushed mine again before finding their way to my neck.

"I'll buy you another for Christmas," he whispered against my throat. His hands explored deeper and lower, ripping the sweater. It was now an official casualty.

My breath rasped at the welcome invasion, and I hooked a finger over Bub's belt as he nudged me backward into the bathroom.

The molten light of dusk filtered through frosted glass skylights, giving the room a red haze. Bub's cologne lingered in the air, along with the humid warmth of a recent shower. I closed my eyes and breathed in the familiar aphrodisiac. The sensations it conjured were a paradox—or maybe just two sides of the same coin—one part tender devotion and the other raw exhilaration.

By the time Bub finished shredding my sweater, I'd managed to unfasten both of our jeans. He paused to drag mine down my legs and threw them across the room before lifting me onto the edge of the counter. One hand went to the mirror behind me, and his other pressed into the small of my back, drawing my body flush with his. I sucked in an eager breath, anticipating what came next.

There were rare few things that could blot out the troubles of the world from my mind, but this was by far my favorite method. Every thrust and kiss, every graze of teeth and bite of nails, was a reminder that we were alive—and together.

At the end of the day, that was still the thing that mattered the most.

After returning from our escape into carnal oblivion, Bub filled the clawfoot tub, adding Epsom salt and bath oils. He waited until I'd settled between his legs before letting reality slip back in.

"Dare I ask how the soul search went today?" he said, reaching for the shampoo. "I assume you found an original believer if demons were afoot."

"Uh, sort of."

"Sort of?" Tension bled through Bub's confused chuckle.

I folded my hands over my eyes and sighed. "I'm pretty sure we found Judas, but then hellcats attacked, and Tasha Henry snapped up the soul before we left the mortal side."

"Tasha Henry? The rebel reaper you risked everything to save? That Tasha Henry?"

"Yes," I snapped. "That one."

Bub clicked his forked tongue. "I don't suppose you need to hear it again, but I'll say it anyway. That bird is bad news, through and through. You should let the council have her."

"Trust me, I would have, had I found her at either of her usual haunts." I leaned forward so he could massage the shampoo into my scalp and wrapped a hand around his scarred calf. "What about you? Any luck with Una last night?"

"As you can probably imagine, she was positively horrid. She mentioned your oath never to return and suggested that an envoy also voided the agreement. I made it very clear that my visit was not at your behest, though I did offer our home to Morgan, should she be willing to spend a season here in Tartarus as a surrogate until you fetch Tantalus. At which point, Una threatened to have me riddled with arrows if I ever again suggested that Morgan leave Faerie."

"Swell." I pulled my knees up to my chest and let him dip my head back in the water to rinse my hair. He ran his thumb across my cheek, wiping away a spot of foam before stealing a kiss.

"You'll have better luck tomorrow," he said. The pinched skin between his brows suggested he was trying to soothe his fears as much as mine.

"The search has been put on hold," I confessed. "After today's disaster, the council and the Fates need time to decide how to proceed."

"They can't do that." Bub shifted in the tub, sloshing water over the edge. The panic that had sent him off on a tangent the night before seemed to be rearing its head again.

"They're considering loaning us Dionysus and the Maenad in the meantime."

"How is that any better than wild hellcats?"

"It's not," I agreed. "I hate to admit it, but Tantalus is the lesser evil in this case."

"Well, regardless, it's good to have a backup plan." Bub relaxed and pulled my back against his chest.

I didn't have the heart to remind him there was no guarantee a surrogate would fix the problem. But that worry could wait. It wasn't something we could solve right now anyway. Besides, I had smaller fish to fry.

"Do me a favor?" I asked, tilting my head back to nuzzle Bub's beard.

"Anything, love."

"Give Rupert an attaboy for dinner. He's trying so hard to impress you, and you're not giving him a fair chance."

"Tricksy vixen," Bub grumbled and nipped my earlobe. "Fine. I'll tell him well done—which is likely the state of this dreadful Welly we're about to choke down."

"Be nice." I splashed a handful of water in his face. Bub caught my wrist and kissed a fiery line down my arm into the bend of my elbow.

"How nice?" he whispered, his free hand caressing my stomach beneath the bathwater. The sharp tang of lust quickened my pulse. The crisis de jour called for more than a countertop quickie, I decided.

"Finish your dinner without complaining, and you can have dessert."

"Something sinfully delicious, I hope." His beard tickled my skin as his kisses migrated to my neck.

"So decadent, you'll need another bath," I promised.

CHAPTER SEVENTEEN

"There are two ways to live: you can live as if nothing is a miracle; you can live as if everything is a miracle."
—Albert Einstein

OPTIMISTIC WASN'T THE RIGHT word for how I felt come Saturday morning. Even hopeful seemed too generous. Satiated, maybe? Quelled?

It was on the tip of my tongue, much like my demon had been the night before. My endorphin-muddled brain refused to focus on bigger questions, especially while I enjoyed coffee on the stink-free patio with Bub. Along with a fresh blueberry scone, courtesy of our proud butler.

Dinner had been amazing. Even my demon had requested a second helping. Which meant that Rupert was in an especially good mood today. Not only had he woken early to bake breakfast pastries, but he'd also scheduled grooming appointments for the hounds and had spot-treated my leather jacket with conditioner.

The workday started on a high note despite my recent demotion. It wasn't until I'd made it through the carnage of a hospital harvest in New York City that the doom and gloom sank its hooks back into me. To be fair, an overcrowded ICU could do that to the best of us. Tallying up NCH souls to pass off to the Lost Souls Unit wasn't exactly great for morale either.

Jenni had said the Posy Unit was backed up, but… *damn.* They were up to their eyeballs in souls. I sent Kevin and Eliza ahead to make a few early deliveries to the afterlives over our lunch break. The ship had a sizable hold, and it'd served me well when I was captain of the Posy Unit, but it had filled up fast today.

Overtime felt like a way of life for all reapers lately, but the Posies already dealt with large quantities of souls. Stepping it up a notch for them was a bit more involved with cargo space limitations and excessive paperwork from their numerous trips across the sea.

Kevin and Eliza wouldn't like me for it, but I tracked down Arden at a funeral home in Memphis and offered to take on a few more harvests. It wasn't like I had anything better to do until the council and the Fates figured out their next move—if that decision even included me.

My short stint as the golden child seemed to have come to an end. It shouldn't have bothered me so much, seeing as how I hadn't wanted the responsibility in the first place. But I also didn't want hellcats to become par for the grave. An apocalypse didn't sound like much fun either.

"I was surprised that President Fang assigned you to help us today," Arden said. "This is not an ideal environment for young apprentices right now." He stopped beside a raised casket and lifted his hand, moving it in a circular motion over the glossy wood. With each pass, his fingers became more translucent until he was finally able to plunge his arm through the casket's closed lid.

"My apprentices can handle medium-risk if I'm there to supervise," I said, taking a careful step back as he yanked a soul out by the scruff of their neck. The man flailed about like a catfish caught by a noodler, but Arden didn't let go until he'd pulled him clear of the casket.

"Where am I?" the soul demanded, taking in all the wreaths and flowers. The service hadn't begun yet, though I heard weeping coming from the next room over.

Arden pointed a finger like the Ghost of Christmas Yet to Come, directing the soul to a podium with a stack of programs. Considering the Posies' tight schedule, it was a wonder he even allowed that much.

"I do appreciate your help," Arden said once the man had wandered off to read the highlights of his life. "But you should know, Molly and Trevor were on a medium-risk harvest when they got attacked. Before that, we only encountered hellcats on high-risk assignments."

"Have you seen a lot of them?" I asked.

"I've seen enough." Arden's brows knit, and he shot his catch a cautious glance. "You know I don't put much stock in rumors, but I overheard that Special Ops might be making a return with the intent to solve the hell breach crisis."

"It's… a touch more complicated than that." I gave him an apologetic smile. Blabbering council business was how I'd screwed the pooch to begin with. Not that I believed Arden would turn on me the way Tasha had. Still, I'd learned my lesson.

"It usually is," Arden said. "Either way, your success is our success, and I wish you well."

"Thanks." I nodded across the room to where the soul was trying to read the card tucked down inside a potted peace lily. "Is this your last one here?"

"Yes, but you're welcome to join me at the children's hospital on the other side of the city. That's where I'm headed after I drop off Mr. Thornton."

"Sure thing," I said, forcing a smile to hide my cringe.

Child souls weren't my cup of death. They reminded me too much of Winston and Naledi, who had both died young on the mortal side before I harvested them. But I'd already volunteered myself, and I had too much respect for Arden to back out now.

He retrieved his digital docket and transferred a list of names to mine. I accepted the file and waved my docket in farewell before coining off to get a head start.

If I were lucky, I'd have just enough time to grab a cup of coffee before heading over to the Woke Souls' winter festival.

Cordelia hadn't mentioned anything about a plus one for the late-night party, but I had a feeling she wouldn't appreciate me showing up with an uninvited demon. Not that that had kept Bub from pleading and pouting this morning when I shared the reason I'd be late coming home tonight.

I expected a fly to hitch a ride across the sea with me. I just hoped he wouldn't get squashed by a perceptive soul, though Bub would have no one to blame but himself.

As the day drew to a close, a sudden panic caught me off guard. I had no idea what I was walking into tonight. No clue what to wear or whether I should bring a gift of some sort to show my gratitude—like maybe a bottle of wine for the hostess. But did Woke Souls even drink wine? Would the gift violate some embargo of which I was unaware?

Maybe a bag of coffee would be safer, I decided as I arrived at the Phantom Café. I nearly changed my mind again when I spotted Ellen Aries. She sat in a booth by herself, bloodshot eyes staring through the front windows and up at the darkening sky. Before I could remove myself from her line of sight, her gaze dropped to where I stood frozen on the sidewalk, one hand hovering over the handle of the front door. Ellen looked away quickly, turning her focus to her cup of coffee.

Remorse stabbed at my heart. I gritted my teeth and entered the café.

Ellen's curls were in better shape than they'd been the last time I saw her, now pinned up in victory rolls that didn't quite go with the exhausted circles under her eyes. When I stopped at her table, her cheeks flushed with humiliation as if she expected me to rip her a new one.

"I heard about Abe," I said, touching her shoulder. "I'm so sorry."

Ellen's bottom lip trembled. "I'm sorry, too. I shouldn't have blown up on you like that. I was just tired and frustrated—I still am. I've been volunteering most nights at Meng's infirmary."

"Oh, wow." I blew out a long sigh as Jenni's words came back to bite me in the ass.

We can only do what we can do.

But there *was* something more I could do.

Ellen rubbed her eyes and yawned before continuing. "Duster spontaneously combusted while I was away last week, and I'm worried sick for Ross."

"That's... a lot." I slipped onto the bench across from her. "For what it's worth, I do want to help. Maybe I could volunteer with you at the infirmary." I stopped shy of offering to feed her cantankerous pet toy phoenix.

"Don't run yourself into the ground like I have." Ellen reached across the table and patted my hand. "I can sleepwalk my way through low-risk harvests. But you need to stay sharp if you're going after souls that attract hellcats. I saw Gabriel at the academy yesterday," she added under her breath.

I guessed he hadn't changed out of his blood-splattered clothes before bringing the spear to Jack. It must have made for quite an entrance.

"They called off the search party for the time being," I said, pausing to give a waitress my order. "Of the three dozen souls the Fates have sent us after, only one was viable." I shook my head as Ellen's eyes widened. "Tasha Henry snatched it up while the hellcats had us distracted."

"*Ooh*, there's a bad egg if there ever was one."

I was plenty ticked at Tasha myself, but hearing others write her off still rubbed me wrong. *Was* she a bad egg? A bad-news bird, as Bub had suggested? Or in

Jenni's opinion, an exiled rebel without a cause turned apocalyptic threat to Eternity?

What reason did Tasha have to trust Jenni or the council? Or me, for that matter? Sure, I'd saved her from being terminated, but I couldn't deny that at least half my motivation had been to appease my own guilt. And what kind of life had she had since then? What other options did she have? What skill set could she rely on?

A waitress delivered my peppermint latte and the bag of pre-ground beans I'd decided to gift Cordelia and company. While she was at our table, she also topped off Ellen's mug and left a tent menu that featured the soup specials and holiday desserts. Not that she needed to. The smell of clam chowder and gingerbread filled the café, and my mouth hadn't stopped watering since I entered the building.

It probably didn't help that I'd skipped lunch to help Arden collect leukemia patients all afternoon. At least he'd spared me the resentment of my apprentices by taking the full lot of souls aboard the boat he shared with his sailing partner, Asha. The child souls were sure to enjoy the carousel bolted to their deck far more than the tattered board games I kept in the hold of my ship.

If I stayed on with Arden's crew, I'd have to hunt down a merry-go-round or a bouncy house or something. They didn't get as many kids as the Mother Goose

Unit, but I didn't want to make a name for myself as the boring Posy.

I quietly sipped my latte and listened to Ellen detail what the past few weeks had been like for her, working alongside Jai Ling—Meng Po's protégé—changing wound dressings and fixing meals. She'd also helped Ross make arrangements for an upcoming mass memorial for the fallen guards.

I'd thought taking the time to offer a sympathetic ear would make me feel better. Instead, I felt like an even bigger schmuck. If the council didn't send me out to search for original believers again soon, I'd have to go with Ellen to the infirmary. If I didn't, my conscience would eat me alive.

The streetlights outside our window flickered to life, and I checked my watch.

"I have to go," I said, not offering a reason. I'd spilled enough beans for one night.

"Thanks for listening to me vent," Ellen said as I stood.

I gave her a weak smile and gathered up my bag of dark roast. "Sounds like you needed it."

She tilted her cup in silent agreement. "Catch you on the flip side."

"Not if I catch you first," I replied with a wink before dropping enough coin on the table to cover her coffee, too.

I was running behind, but I expected there was a bit of wiggle room where *twilight* was concerned. Either way, mending fences with old friends would always be worth arriving fashionably late.

CHAPTER EIGHTEEN

"Listen; there's a hell of a good universe next door: let's go."
—*e. e. cummings*

THE WIND BLOWING OFF the sea was bitter cold. It slapped at my face and hair and made my teeth chatter as I steered my tender around the Isles of Eternity, looking for a safe spot to land in the fading daylight.

The scarf and gloves I'd pilfered from an old trunk that Josie had kept aboard our ship offered little relief, but I wore them more for moral support than anything else. I wondered what she would think of all this if she were here, and my heart twinged with regret that she wasn't and couldn't talk it over with me.

There were seven islands in all, but no one knew for certain how many were inhabited. The largest of the isles, where I'd witnessed the first souls crawling out of the sea, was a given. Torches to guide sea travelers away from danger lined the beaches. The other six isles didn't have much beach area to speak of, but the big island's lights were bright enough to illuminate them all.

With Cordelia's invitation directing me to the north-ernmost isle, I assumed that one was occupied, too, at the very least. She'd mentioned a village, and what was a village without villagers?

Yet even in the near dark, I didn't see any lights beyond the thick forest butted up against the shoreline. I cruised around the isle twice before the faint outline of a man caught my attention. He stood on a narrow stretch of beach, a torch in one hand and his other pointing out the entrance of a gravel bar that curled inland.

I throttled down the tender's motor, then killed it as the hull scraped bottom.

"You made it," the man shouted in greeting. He thrust his torch into the sand and rushed to help me pull the boat ashore. "We were afraid you might not come," he said breathlessly, then bubbled with laughter as he gave me another once-over. "Everyone is so excited to meet you. I'm Gavin, by the way."

I shook his hand and glanced down at his rolled-up jeans and bare feet. "Aren't you cold?"

"Huh?" His gaze followed mine to his bluish toes, and he wiggled them in the wet gravel. "Oh, sure. But it's warmer in the village. You'll see." He fetched the torch and waved his arm, bidding me to follow him toward a narrow path set between two trees. I hadn't noticed it from the water.

I tucked the bag of ground coffee under one arm and retied my scarf as I trailed after Gavin. Even if it were warmer in the village, it was still freezing on the coast.

Once we were out of the wind and shielded by thick evergreens on all sides, sensation began to return to my ears and fingertips. I yanked off my gloves and rubbed my hands together, sighing with relief. The air was sweeter here, a perfume of pine and cypress laced with lavender, ginseng, rosemary, and dill. I'd anticipated the trees, but I hadn't expected much else to grow on the isles in the dead of winter.

"We call this the Harvian Wood," Gavin said. He shot me a shy smile over his shoulder and pointed a finger at the trees all around us.

"What?" I blinked at him and then up at the dark canopy above. "Why?"

"After you, of course."

I stopped in the middle of the path. Gavin took a few more steps before he noticed and backtracked.

"Are you okay?" At my stunned silence, he added, "Was it something I said? If it's about the forest name, we already have the Lana Lagoon. That's why we went with your last name."

"Oh," I said, as if it all suddenly made sense, and I wasn't having a minor meltdown over learning that the Woke Souls had gone geography happy with my name.

Once again, I wondered what the hell I was walking into. An episode of the Twilight Zone seemed all too plausible. And when had the temperature spiked from Antarctica to Amazonia?

Gavin opened his free arm as I stripped out of my scarf and jacket. "Can I carry any of that for you?" he asked.

"I'm fine," I said, waving him off. "I just need… a minute to catch my breath." *In case things get any weirder and I have to make a mad dash back to my boat*, I silently added.

"You sure I can't take some of that off your hands?" Gavin frowned at everything I was carrying. "I'll never hear the end of it if I show up with the guest of honor loaded down like a pack mule."

"Well, we can't have that." I turned over the scarf and jacket but kept the coffee. I wanted to give it to Cordelia personally, so I could ask her why she'd failed to mention all these extra details. I also wanted to know if the council was aware of my celebrity status on the isles. It didn't seem like a pill they'd have an easy time swallowing. I was still choking on it myself.

"It's not much farther," Gavin said, stealing another backward glance as he continued down the path. There was more worry than admiration in his eyes now. As if he were aware that he had overshared—or knew what awaited me ahead.

I shoved the sleeves of my sweater up my arms and reluctantly followed him. Sweat had broken out across my face and chest. Though the air was fragrant, it was humid, and I was having a hard time breathing. The trickle of adrenaline pumping through my veins didn't help.

Voices echoed in the distance, and flickering firelight seeped through the trees. Soon, drums and stringed instruments joined the growing din, along with laughter and singing.

"She's here!" someone shouted.

I froze again, but Gavin had reached the end of the path. He stepped aside, letting the scene unfold for me in the clearing beyond.

Hundreds of souls turned to stare at me. They were dressed in scraps of mismatched clothes that spanned the past few centuries, and most were barefoot like Gavin. They reveled around three bonfires that burned in a row down the center of the clearing. Small log cabins and huts pressed up against the forest along the outskirts of the space. Tables made of more roughhewn wood were scattered in front of the tiny homes, filled with food and drink.

Cordelia emerged from the throng and opened her arms to me with a wide smile. "Welcome to the winter festival, Lana."

With my identity confirmed, the crowd erupted. My name was in every mouth, tinged with excitement and awe. Someone whistled, and several others began chanting. A sobbing woman touched my arm as Cordelia led me away toward one of the cabins.

"Let's get you into some more breathable clothes," she said. "You can change back in the morning."

"Oh, I can't stay all night," I insisted, my throat tightening with another dose of panic. "I have to work tomorrow."

"Don't worry. A little throne water should fix you right up." Her cryptic smile was beginning to unnerve me, but before I could inquire what the hell throne water was, she asked, "Are you still searching for original believers to mend the compromised hells?"

It seemed like something she should have already known the answer to, but then again, I was sure the rest of the council didn't invite her to every meeting. They were elitists, after all. Even the subservient beings didn't regard souls with the same respect as their own kind.

"I guess you didn't hear about the incident with Judas yesterday." I winced, trying to decide how to break the news of my failure to the leader of my new fan club.

"Oh, I heard," Cordelia said, entering the cabin ahead of me. "But I assumed you, of all deities, wouldn't let the council slow you down."

"Well, I—wait, what?" I stopped inside the doorway. "Did you say deity?"

"I did. We're all here because of you. What else could you be?" Cordelia asked.

"I don't know what you've been told, and I can't even begin to fathom who would say such a thing, but I'm just a reaper."

"Just a reaper." She chuckled and opened a primitive-looking wardrobe in the corner of the cabin's single room. The clothes inside hung on hangers fashioned from bound twigs and consisted of primarily solid-colored, sleeveless dresses.

"I thought you turned down the visa proposal," I said. "Has one of the charities in Limbo City been donating food and clothes?"

"We have a farm on the big island," Cordelia explained. "In addition to a wide variety of produce, we have chickens, goats, and sheep. One of the Woke Souls built a loom and makes additional clothing for us, though most still favor their enlightenment attire—the clothes they were wearing the day you woke us."

"That was the throne, not me." I shook my head, refusing to accept credit for a feat that had nearly killed me and hadn't even been my idea. Naledi's disembodied voice had directed me to the sea. I'd released the throne's power because it had hurt too much to hold it. If I hadn't, it likely would have destroyed me.

"You're too modest." Cordelia's smile softened. "It's a rare and noble trait for a goddess."

"Goddess?" I snorted out a dry laugh. This was ridiculous. "I told you, it was the throne."

"We do not praise the blade that slays the dragon," Cordelia said. "We give our gratitude to the warrior who wields the weapon. That's you, Lana. Let us thank you. I think you'll be quite pleased with your reward."

"Reward?" I felt like a parrot, echoing these strange words that my brain refused to grasp back at her.

"That's why you're here, isn't it?" Cordelia's grin returned.

"No," I said, my face scrunching with offense. "I just came to... give you this." I thrust the bag of coffee at her. "And to officially welcome you to Eternity. That's all."

Cordelia accepted the coffee without taking her eyes from me. "But you've already given us so much. It's our turn to give back."

"I don't know what more to say," I admitted. "This is a lot to process, and I sincerely don't need any reward."

"Don't you, though?" Cordelia pulled a white dress from the wardrobe and handed it to me. "What do you desire most right now?"

"Definitely some cooler clothes," I said, accepting the garment. "Thank you, this is perfect."

"And beyond that?" Cordelia's brows hitched, and her lips pressed into a tight line. She was getting frustrated with me. Whatever game we were playing, I was losing. But no one had told me the rules.

"What do I desire most right now?" I fell back into parrot mode, repeating the question. Honesty was easy when she clearly already knew the answer. "Original believers that can fix the broken borders of the underworld and stop hellcats from escaping," I answered bluntly. "Got any of those hidden in the back of your wardrobe?"

"Well, maybe not in the wardrobe." Cordelia's eyes twinkled. "Change your clothes, and then we'll see what we can see."

She patted my arm and left the cabin to give me some privacy. I waited until I was alone before dropping onto a chair beside her bed. My legs felt like spaghetti. I wasn't sure if that had more to do with the suffocating heat or the idea that she might actually be harboring an original believer on the island. It didn't seem possible.

The Isles of Eternity sheltered atheists and agnostics. How could an original believer have ended up here? How would Cordelia even recognize one or tell who they had been in a past life? And would knowing the answer to that put me in a sticky situation with the council? Would they see me as some sort of accomplice to the Woke Souls' hidden agenda?

Whatever long-term consequences awaited, Cordelia's preface detailed how this was my reward: this thing I desired most. Which led me to believe that if she *did* have an original believer on the island, they would turn it over to me. I would be able to take the soul directly to their designated hell and place a late-night tea order with Jack.

The thought made my fingers tremble with anticipation. I undressed in a rush, draping my clothes over the back of the chair before donning the white dress. I was taller than Cordelia by a few inches, so the hemline hit me just below the knee, leaving a few inches of skin above the tops of my boots. I considered leaving them on, but it felt rude somehow with everyone else wandering around barefoot. I pulled them off, along with my socks, and tucked them under the chair.

The dirt floor felt cool beneath my feet, instantly dropping my body to a more comfortable temperature. My mood eased with the sudden relief, and I exited the cabin feeling surer of myself. Until the souls turned on me again.

"This way," Cordelia said, directing me through the crowd of celebrating souls. Hands reached out, brushing my arms as I walked past. They didn't grab or pinch, so I tolerated it without complaining. It was no more intrusive than being jostled about on the busy sidewalks of Limbo City.

Cordelia slipped away from the halos of the bonfires and led me toward another hidden path through the forest. The trail was shorter this time, leading farther inland. The light that greeted us through the trees was different, too, glowing an eerie blue.

Soon, we reached our destination. It was a pond—no, a lagoon.

"The Lana Lagoon," Gavin said. I turned and found him and a few other souls on the path behind me.

"Why does it glow like that?" I asked, looking back at the sparkling water.

Gavin shrugged. "We just assumed you made it that way."

There'd been no room in my head for shimmery pools of blue water when I dumped the throne's power into the sea. There had hardly been room for my own name. Gavin held some Bob Ross version of me in his mind that didn't exist, leisurely painting happy little trees and sandy beaches. But trying to dismiss the significance of the role I'd played in creating the islands or waking the souls was proving pointless.

Cordelia waded into the lagoon, the electric hue painting blue highlights and shadows across her dress and face. She held out her hands, inviting us to join her. Gavin offered me his hand, and I accepted it in spite of myself. The hopeful, naïve expression on his face was breaking my heart. I could just tell I would end up letting them all down.

The water in the lagoon was cold and salty. I smelled the bite of the sea wafting off the surface as I stepped in, though the trees bowing over us formed a cocoon of warm air. The contrast reminded me of the peculiar space between realms that was neither here nor there, the metaphysical veil I was drawn through each time I rolled a coin.

"You feel it, don't you?" Cordelia reached out and took my free hand.

"I don't know what I feel," I said. I followed that up more openly with, "But I feel *something*."

"The sea has given us many gifts," Cordelia said. "It holds many yet, and with the difficulty you've encountered in your search for the necessary souls to restore balance to Eternity, I expect one is waiting to be found here."

The three other souls that had followed us down the path entered the water, taking up posts between Cordelia and Gavin. They linked hands, completing our circle. And then I *really* felt it. Whatever *it* was.

The icy lagoon bubbled with intent, and the silty bottom worked its way between my toes. When I looked back up at Cordelia, her eyes glowed as blue as the water. So did Gavin's, and those of everyone else gathered with us.

"The throne is still yours to wield," Cordelia whispered. "You need only tell it what you desire. With your heart," she clarified as my mouth gaped open and all intelligent thought escaped me.

What if the sea didn't hold either of the remaining souls? Would the lagoon cough up enough stones to spell out: *Better luck next time*?

I tried to shrug off my doubt and focus. This went far beyond some magic eight ball.

Tantalus and Zaynab remained. They were both vital, but the latter would alleviate Khadija's suffering. Before I had a chance to string the request together in my mind, the water in the lagoon churned and gurgled. A whirlpool twisted in the center of our circle, and a liquid form that soon took the shape of a woman with dark hair and sharp eyes rose from it. Her long gown dragged in the water around her legs.

When the lagoon settled, Cordelia broke the circle to take the woman's hand and stroked her arm. "What's your name, dear?"

"Zaynab," the woman replied, taking in the lush forest enclosing us. "Is this... Shamayim?" She seemed confused, as if she hadn't expected paradise to be waiting for her. Unfortunately, it wasn't.

"No," Cordelia answered gently.

"You're needed elsewhere," I said, still working out how to explain the situation. I could hardly understand it myself. Zaynab was right in front of me, her past lives inexplicably melted away by the throne and the sea. "You've been selected for a job of sorts," I tried again. "A queenhood, really. You'll be generously compensated."

I would have taken her to Jahannam kicking and screaming, if necessary, but willing souls were always more pleasant to work with.

Gavin and the others formed a protective circle around Zaynab. For a second, my heart dropped at the fear that they might not let me take her. But as Cordelia linked her arm with mine, directing me toward the shore and the path back into the village, they fell into step behind us.

"When the council asks how you came by this soul, I think it would be in everyone's best interest if you left out the finer details," she said. I would have claimed that I had found the soul in a dumpster behind a dreidel factory if it meant getting her in my boat and coined off to Jahannam before dawn.

"What should I tell the council?" I asked Cordelia.

"The simple truth. That the sea washed away her past lives, and you found her in the water while visiting the isles. A coincidence."

A whisper of a laugh escaped me. "No, meeting you was a coincidence. This is nothing short of a miracle."

"*You* are the miracle, Lana." Cordelia squeezed my hand. "You still don't see it, but you will."

CHAPTER NINETEEN

"I saw a study that said speaking in front of a crowd is
considered the number one fear of the average person.
Number two was death. This means to the average person,
if you have to be at a funeral, you would rather be
in the casket than doing the eulogy."
—Jerry Seinfeld

THOUGH I HADN'T PLANNED TO, I did end up spending the night on the northern isle with the Woke Souls. I felt obligated after they'd practically handed me the Jahannam soul on a silver platter. No matter how many times Cordelia explained that I'd been the one to accomplish the act, I couldn't view myself as anything more than a reaper. Even when the celebrating souls dragged me into the infinity loop they danced around the bonfires.

At first, I'd resisted. But soon, I found myself delirious with joy, laughing hard enough to draw tears. Their good cheer and appreciation were infectious and every bit as enchanting as a faerie ring. Except when the Woke

Souls were done with me, I felt invigorated. Like I could take on the universe and maybe even win.

Bub's stowaway spy tickled the back of my ear throughout the night, remaining nestled in the small hollow behind my lobe. I could only imagine what my demon would have to say when I returned home, though it would have to wait.

As the first light of dawn broke the sky above the Harvian Wood, the music tapered off, and the souls said their goodbyes before disappearing inside the cabins and huts that surrounded the clearing. Cordelia brought my jacket and scarf to me as I finished lacing my boots.

"Gavin is waiting at your boat with the soul," she said.

"Thank you. For everything."

"Thank *you*." Cordelia grinned. "I'm sure it goes without saying, but I'll make it official in case you have any doubt. You're welcome back anytime."

I nodded, unable to speak past the lump in my throat. Of course I wanted to come back. Hell, I didn't want to leave. There was something about the isle that felt more like home than Limbo City or Tartarus ever had, and it wasn't just because the souls had named the forest and lagoon after me.

But I had a life and a job to get back to. I had apprentices to train and hellhounds to spoil, an angel to rib and a demon to love. This place could never be home. It just wasn't in the cards.

I dug my cell phone out of my pocket and scrolled through my contacts until I found Maalik's number. As the council representative for Jahannam, he was the right person to contact. Still, my stomach knotted. He would have questions that I couldn't answer. But he was also the only person I knew who was familiar with the Islamic hell and where Zaynab would be staying.

I took a deep breath and pressed the call button. He answered on the first ring.

"Lana?" Leave it to Maalik to remember my number even when I hadn't dialed him in over a decade. "Is everything all right?" he asked, concern hitching his voice.

"How soon can you meet me at the gates of Jahannam?"

"Why?"

"I have a gift for Khadija," I said.

"Give me ten minutes."

"I'll see you soon." I hung up without offering more information. I was too afraid he'd share the news with Ridwan, his grumpy, angelic colleague on the council. This would be complicated enough with one feathered asshole in the mix.

Jahannam's gates had mostly been defunct since the Abrahamic faiths decided to join forces and utilize a single gateway for the incoming sinners. It seemed like a good, quiet spot to hand off the soul without drawing too much attention.

When I arrived with Zaynab, Maalik was already waiting—along with Iblis, an Islamic devil who ruled a large territory of Jahannam with his court of djinn followers.

"I guess we won't be needing Lady Meng's services this morning," Maalik said, taking in the soul with wide eyes. His wings shuddered, and he gave me a curious frown, but he kept whatever questions he had to himself as Iblis welcomed Zaynab.

"Well, aren't you a lovely creature?" he said, luring her away from me with compliments and open arms. His attention cut briefly to me, and he beamed with gratitude. "I'll take good care of her," he promised. "My servants have already prepared a lavish wing in the palace. You can come see for yourself if you'd like."

"I'll take your word for it." I gave him a tight smile, hoping he wouldn't take offense at my refusal. When it came to the underworlds, I preferred my own slice of the inferno.

"Maybe another time," Maalik said when Iblis extended the same offer to him. "We really should be going. The council will want to receive Lana's report personally."

"Right," I squeaked, hoping he'd only said that to get me off the hook with Iblis. But I should have known better.

Maalik's hand found my elbow as we parted ways with the devil and his entourage of djinn servants. I bristled at the gesture. As if sensing my discomfort, Bub's tiny spy buzzed away from my ear and into the angel's, sending him reeling away from me.

I tried and failed to hide a satisfied smirk until a line of smoking hellfire shot from Maalik's fingertip, baking the fly to a crisp. It dropped to the ground, twitching and sizzling.

"Hey!" I yanked my arm away as Maalik reached for me again. "Hands to yourself, and no roasting my bodyguards."

"And you thought *I* was jealous." He shook his head as Bub's *Sympathy for the Devil* ringtone blew up my phone. I rolled my eyes and accepted the call.

"That wasn't me," I blurted. "But I'm heading to Reapers Inc. next, so you won't be able to follow anyway."

Bub snorted. "Regardless, if the Keeper of Hellfire can't keep his mitts off my *goddess*, I'll gladly relieve him of them."

"Love you, too. Kiss-kiss," I said, opting to distance Maalik with cringeworthy cuteness rather than threats. The angel rolled his eyes and stalked off toward the coin zone outside the gates.

"Be careful," Bub said, sensing my unease. "The council could see this new development as an instrument at their disposal or as a threat."

"I'd prefer they not know about this new development *at all*," I said under my breath.

"Yes, that would be best," he agreed. "And I do love you. Be careful."

"Always."

We said goodbye, and I took a moment to steel my nerves before catching up to Maalik.

"I didn't know the fly belonged to your demon consort," he said, gritting his teeth through the half-assed apology. Khadija was in the clear, and *that* was the best he could muster?

"Sure you didn't." I checked my watch before glancing out at the sea beyond the rocky coastline. A crystal-clear morning lit up the sky. The day was off to a lovely start. And now, Maalik and his cohorts were about to spoil it.

"Shall we?" he said, amicably opening his hand in invitation.

I sighed and fetched my coin from my pocket. "Let's get this over with."

Standing in front of the council after all this time felt a lot like stepping in hellhound crap and forgetting to wipe off my boot until after I'd tracked it all through the house. Only I didn't have a demon butler to help me clean up this mess.

Parvati tapped the nails of both of her left hands on the conference table. She hadn't spoken a word, but her sharp eyes spelled out her disbelief well enough. Besides, Ridwan was managing the inquisition just fine on his own.

"You mean to tell us that you just *happened* upon this soul, and she just *happened* to be fully stripped of her past lives?" he demanded for the third time.

"Did you just *happen* to forget I've already answered this question?" I snapped. Losing my patience with the council was never a smart move, but I'd expected more congratulations than scrutiny, and so far, they were coming up short.

"In other news," said Cindy Morningstar, the last person I expected to save me from this redundant conversation, "Hell has paid the ransom Ms. Henry requested, and Judas has been secured. He's settling in at the Inferno Chateau as we speak."

"Bravo," the Green Man said, clapping his hands. He had offered me no such praise, but I swallowed my disappointment. It wasn't worth getting sucked back into the fray.

"That just leaves Tartarus," Athena said, her gaze shifting from me to Jenni and then to Hecate, who had propped herself in a corner of the room after a brief spat with Gabriel over who would take the remaining seat at the table.

"And the hoard of hellcats terrorizing the mortal side," Gabriel said. "We have a new lead on the situation."

"Careful, cherub." Hecate seethed behind him, her eyes glinting with wrath. "Official accusations have official consequences."

Gabriel snorted. "While I'm not entirely convinced that you're *not* somehow linked to the apocalypse, I've identified the lion-faced beast among the hellcats. Professor Jackson had a look at the mark on the spear we recovered, and it's of Sumerian origin. The star of Inanna. Making the creature with the scorpion tail—"

"Ninurta's mount." Parvati gasped. "Of course."

Kwan Yin nodded. "Though he is likely not involved with this latest coup. He returned to the mortal coil shortly after losing his mace."

The eyes in the room shifted toward me again, and I sank lower in my chair. I hadn't *meant* to obliterate Sharur, the smasher of thousands. But the enhanced weapon had gone to the dark side, and it was either it or us. Warren's tracking missile chose *us*.

"The spearhead is newer than the staff attached to it," Gabriel continued. "So, we're likely looking at a servant of Inanna's, possibly her vizier, Ninshubur."

Parvati's nails set to tapping again. "If she is searching for original believers, she must have a plan."

"She wants the throne," Cindy Morningstar interjected. "We should seize it before she has the chance."

The room exploded as everyone tried to offer their opinions on the subject all at once. My name began making the rounds, but I couldn't follow who suggested what, only that they were willing to force my compliance if necessary.

They can try, I thought darkly, wondering what pulling an angel like Ridwan out of existence would feel like. Or a demon princess like Cindy Morningstar. The fire that heralded my wrathful talent stirred in my chest.

"One crisis at a time," Athena shouted, raising her hand to quiet everyone. "I understand the Fates have given Hecate a new list. Let's see if that will seal the borders of the underworld before we get ahead of ourselves with hypothetical solutions to the throne issue."

"Yes, let's," Hecate said, pushing away from the conference room wall and placing a cool hand on my shoulder. "Come along, reaper. I promise not to bewitch your hounds this time."

CHAPTER TWENTY

*"I hold it to be the inalienable right of anybody
to go to hell in his own way."*
—*Robert Frost*

THE FATES' NEW LIST boiled down to a single stop. The thirteen names all belonged to the same coven in Minneapolis, and they were having a ritual tonight—with a human sacrifice.

"Leave it to Tantalus," I mused as we waited atop a picnic table in a forgotten corner of a state park. "Please tell me these witches of yours aren't cannibals."

"They used to eat dogs," Hecate confessed. "But not humans."

"Joy." I shuddered and silently thanked Khadija that my hounds were invisible to mortal eyes. Saul and Coreen patrolled the perimeter of the clearing where the witches were due to arrive at any moment. Gabriel and the only two nephilim guards Ross could spare had taken up perches in the higher trees, keeping a lookout for hell-cats and Ninurta's nightmare of a hybrid mount.

"I should have known that Inanna was behind this." Hecate sighed and reclined on her elbows, the long sleeves of her robe dragging across the splintered tabletop. She'd skipped her modern business attire in favor of traditional ritual wear tonight since it was one of the rare occasions when her most loyal disciples would see her. "She tried to take over several of the underworlds during the First War," Hecate explained. "She even went after her sister's domain."

That didn't sound so out of the ordinary for the old gods and their old ways, but I kept my mouth shut. I hadn't come along until a thousand-plus years later. What did I know?

"I hope you don't mind, but I'd rather not rub elbows with Tantalus when we're done here," I said, changing the subject to one closer to home.

"Oh, the Fates gave up on that one." Hecate sighed as if she were as relieved as I was by the news. "They found an old friend of mine whom the gods once turned into a polecat. I suspect her original soul won't mind returning to my side in her human form for a change."

"What did she do to earn the wrath of the gods— no, wait. Don't tell me," I said, deciding I was better off not knowing. I could deal with that revelation another day.

"Here they come," Hecate whispered as a line of women dressed in black robes filed into the clearing. The shadows of their hoods hid their eyes, but their mouths moved as they chanted a prayer to Hecate to watch over their sister as she passed through the veil and into the grove. I guessed the goddess hadn't explained that there'd be an Uber ride or two along the way.

As the women set up their altar and began calling the cardinal directions, Hecate's eyes took on the blue sheen that heralded her power. It reminded me of the lagoon water on the northern isle. Whatever spark of soul matter tied her to her followers also darkened the sky. She was a nocturnal goddess, after all. And one whose energy was deeply rooted in the underworld. Which was likely why it attracted hellcats so well.

Gabriel saw them first and shouted a warning cry as the beasts rushed into the clearing. There were so many of them, coming from all directions. And Ninurta's mount led the way. Hecate dragged me off the table just as the creature's stinger splintered through the boards I'd been sitting on.

"Come on!" The goddess dragged me toward the circle of women. "You have to identify the original believer so I know whose soul to sever."

Gabriel's wings hissed against my back as he dropped out of the sky, putting himself between me and the advancing hoard. "'I am in the midst of lions,'" he shouted over the roaring din of wings as hellcats and nephilim struggled in the air above us. "'I am forced to dwell among ravenous beasts,'" he bellowed, reciting the scripture as his battle cry.

Hecate pushed me in front of a robed woman, but her eyes were closed in meditation. This was impossible.

"Hey!" I shouted, remembering the antics I'd been forced to preform throughout our previous searches. "What's that in the sky? A bird?"

One of the women pushed the hood of her robe back and squinted at me—just as a hellcat shoved me to the ground in the middle of the ritual circle. A nephilim swooped out of the sky and skewered the beast on his spear.

My sigh of relief came too soon. A stinger the size of a football stabbed the earth beside my head, throwing dirt in my eyes. I screamed and kicked at the beast's underside.

"Catch!" a guard shouted overhead. I opened my hand in time to catch the spear he dropped, using the handle to bat away the next strike of the stinger. Then I angled the tip at the beast's throat and loosed a war cry as I drove the spear into its heart.

"Rest later, reaper," Hecate hissed as she dragged me upright by one arm. "You're not done yet."

The woman who had seen me now lay across the altar between the other women, her soul glowing faintly beneath the surface of her skin. I ran a trembling hand down her chest and stepped back to watch the same liquid illusion that had taken place in Texas. Only this time, the soul was at peace and ready to depart.

"Come along, dark one," Hecate said, taking the woman by the hand. "The lampads await."

"I hear they host the very best orgies," the woman replied. She groaned and closed her eyes as she threw back her head. "I can't wait to see them again."

I shot Hecate a dirty look. "Well, there goes the neighborhood."

CHAPTER TWENTY-ONE

*"People say, 'But Betty, Facebook is a great way to connect
with old friends.' Well, at my age, if I want to connect with
old friends, I need a Ouija board."*
—*Betty White*

I WAS TOO EXHAUSTED to stick around for the soul-
peeling ceremony at Hades' house, but Jack told me it
went off without a hitch, though Persephone was a bit
disappointed to learn that the new soul would be staying
in Hecate's Grove. All that renovation on the guest
house and no creepy cannibal to enjoy it. What a shame.

I considered taking Monday off, but Arden's unit
was still in a bind, so I took my apprentices on the hospital rounds through Los Angeles and San Francisco,
then Dallas and Miami. It was a long, boring day of un-
exciting deaths. No killer clowns. No ancient beasts of
burden and mayhem. And thank goodness.

Tuesday was shorter, but only because the Nephilim
Guard Memorial was being unveiled in the park. The
bronze statue bore a striking resemblance to Abe,

though it was intended to represent over a hundred guards, all slain by hellcats on the mortal side. Plenty of nephilim still filled the beds at Meng's infirmary, but the death toll had dropped off after Ninurta's stabby-tailed mount had gone the way of the dodo.

After the memorial, there were drinks at Purgatory and then poker night on the ship. Bub broke out the good stuff and kept everyone's glasses full as we played. Of course, it was hard to cheat at poker with sober players. I went all-in after only three hands and excused myself to find a quiet spot above deck where I nursed an Ambrosia Ale and tried to decompress after the crushing weight of the past week.

So, of course, that's when a mischievous little girl in a red dress appeared out of thin air. I sputtered and shot beer out my nose. Morgan giggled as I hacked and coughed.

"Does Una know where you are?" I glared at her, wondering how much trouble I would be in with her faerie queen babysitter.

"Don't you worry about sweet Una," Morgan said. "I won't be long. I just wanted to see how you were faring now that all the excitement has died down. Bub was most insistent you required my council, but I see you've managed just fine on your own."

"Yeah, the borders are sealed up. No more hellcats being summoned to the mortal side."

"I meant the excitement of bonding with your believers," Morgan clarified, nodding toward the isles in the distance.

"Believers?" I hitched an eyebrow. "They're atheists. They don't believe in anything."

"They believe in you, don't they?" Morgan's eyes twinkled, reminding me of Cordelia.

"That's different."

"Not as different as you might think. You're ingrained in their soul matter now, an integral part of their foundation. Can't you feel it calling to you?"

"No." I shook my head. "It's not like that."

Morgan's musical laugh echoed across the harbor. "You're a unique case, Lana Harvey. A warrior and a savior. Half original believer, and half goddess. The first of your kind. Why wouldn't you have a devoted cult of your own?"

"Oh, it's a cult now?"

"Congregation. Sect. Flock." Morgan shrugged. "They're yours. Call them whatever you like."

A cheer filtered up from below deck. Someone had won a large jackpot, which meant that someone else had likely gone all-in.

Morgan sensed that our private meeting was coming to an end, too. She curtseyed and then gave the hollow stone tied around her neck a twist, instantly vanishing.

Something scraped the side of the ship, and then the sea sloshed softly as if an oar had broken the surface.

I peered out into the darkness that stretched beyond the lantern-lit harbor, but whatever charm Morgan had used prevented me from seeing her boat, as well.

My gaze stretched farther, taking in the Isles of Eternity. A light flickered somewhere beyond the trees, and for just a moment, I could have sworn I heard drums and laughter. An invisible string tugged at my heart, begging me to return. Calling me home.

Was Morgan right? Were these souls mine?

It sounded like such a monumental responsibility. But I had enjoyed spending time with them. They were pure and kind and, most of all, content. They had asked for nothing more than the pleasure of my company.

I could give that to them again, couldn't I? Maybe being the resident celebrity wasn't entirely out of the question.

But a goddess? Yeah, right.

Cordelia's Cheshire cat smile danced through my mind.

You still don't see it, but you will.

Return to Limbo City in book 2
Shadow of Death
Available Now!

**What do you get for the goddess
who has everything?** Aside from the skull of her
most prized mortal vessel, that is.

Lana didn't expect an invitation from Isis to the biggest
bash in Duat, but then favors are seldom requested without first greasing the wheels. The goddess needs a
trustworthy reaper for a top-secret mission: to retrieve a
talisman hidden in the tomb of an Egyptian queen before
it's unearthed by archaeologists.

The relic possesses magical properties. In the wrong
hands, it could unleash a plague on humans—or the afterlives. Lana soon discovers scientists are the least of
her worries. If she'd known about the tomb-raiding cult
hellbent on resurrecting Seth, she would have charged
double.

ACKNOWLEDGMENTS

My core team hasn't really changed all that much throughout the years. I know that must make these acknowledgments seem awfully repetitive, but it's really a wonderful feeling. It can be hard finding the right people—in all areas of life. I know how lucky I am to have found my people early on and to still be working with them today.

Special thanks to: my husband Paul, who endures my plot and research ramblings and is always first to proofread everything I write; my son Xavier who understands when I have to put in the long hours and smothers me with much-needed hugs and kisses whenever I take breaks; my critique group the Four Horsemen of the Bookocalypse whose kindness and support goes above and beyond; THE Professor George Shelley, who may be retired but will always hold the honorable title of professor in my book for his invaluable feedback and friendship; Kaitlyn Beck, my cousin and friend, who once again modeled as Lana for the covers of the spin-off series; Chelle Olson, my sweet, patient editor who keeps my prose tidy (all remaining errors are my own and likely ones Chelle advised against); Rebecca Frank, who once again designed the most lovely covers; Hollie Jackson, whom I'm so glad will be voicing Lana again for the audiobook editions; and finally, my Grim Readers, many of whom emailed and messaged countless times to request more adventures for Lana. Thank you from the bottom of my heart. This new series would have never happened without your insistence. I hope you're as thrilled as I am to be back in Limbo City!

ABOUT THE AUTHOR

USA Today bestselling author **Angela Roquet** is a great big weirdo. She lives in Missouri with her husband and son in a house stuffed with books, toys, skulls, owls, and glitter-speckled craft supplies. Angela a member of SFWA and HWA, as well as the Four Horsemen of the Bookocalypse, her epic book critique group, where she's known as Death. When not swearing at the keyboard, she enjoys boating with her family at Lake of the Ozarks and reading books that raise eyebrows.

You can find Angela online at
www.angelaroquet.com

If you enjoyed this book, please leave a review or tell a friend. Your support means so much!